A Sprinkle of Spring

A Sprinkle of Spring

A Silver Falls Romance

Melissa McClone

TULE
PUBLISHING

Dedication

For everyone who fell in love with Silver Falls the way I did.

Special thanks to the team at Tule Publishing—Jane, Meghan, Sinclair, Nikki, and Cyndi—who supported this series in so many ways! I'm very grateful!

Chapter One

A S MUSIC PLAYED and people danced in Margot Winslow's living room, Anna Kent stood at the entrance to the dining room and focused her attention on the three newlywed couples in attendance tonight. Their happiness and love and the real-life heart eyes filled Anna with the warm and fuzzies. She was thrilled for three of her closest friends.

I want that.

Anna's boss, Callie, had married Brandt Winslow this past summer; Taryn had eloped with Callie's brother Garrett; and Raine had married Callie's brother Keaton a little over a week ago. None of Anna's friends had been looking for a boyfriend, yet love found them. Collided right into them, not literally, but close enough. Now each woman was happily married to the man of their dreams and living in Silver Falls.

Anna rubbed a spot of longing over her heart.

That's exactly what I want.

To meet Mr. Right. To fall in love. To live happily ever after. She wanted to ask for a table for two instead of settling for a lone spot at the bar. She wanted to be loved for who she was.

Patience.

Anna repeated the word like a mantra. She needed to be patient about finding the man of her dreams. She'd learned by watching her friends a relationship couldn't be forced. It couldn't be wished for or made to happen. Love happened when a person least expected it, so Anna was trying that—not expecting anything. Instead, she was waiting and hoping, leaving her dating and love life up to chance or fate or whatever else you wanted to call it.

Patience.

She smiled at Mrs. Jones before making her way to the buffet table where appetizers and desserts had been set out.

Her time was coming. That first blush of attraction. The excitement of the first date. The falling into something more. The declaration of love. The full acceptance of her past.

Yep, *he* was out there waiting for her. Somewhere. She hoped somewhere in Silver Falls.

Patience.

Silently, she repeated the word three more times.

Margot sashayed up to the table. She was in her early sixties, or rather, that was what Anna had heard, but Margot was young at heart with an enviable boho style few could pull off. As she shimmied to the beat of the music, the black and gold feather boa fluttered. "Why aren't you dancing?"

"Thought I might check on Milo," Anna said. "He took off with Rex, Autumn, and your dogs as soon as we arrived."

"Sadie and Angus enjoy having friends over. Same as me." Margot's blue eyes twinkled. "Having fun tonight?"

"Once again, you've proven you're Silver Falls's hostess

with the mostest."

"*Moi*?" Margot tossed her boa. "Thank you. Get out on the dance floor. It's almost midnight, and Flynn needs a partner."

Anna's muscles tightened. She would never move in on Pippa's potential boyfriend. Besides, Anna wanted nothing to do with Flynn Andrews. Callie called her oldest brother the arrogant surgeon. She wasn't wrong. But he was Margot's family by marriage, so Anna needed to be polite about the jerk. "I…"

"What, dear?"

"Flynn's with Pippa. The two were attached at the hip at Raine and Keaton's wedding reception. And rumor has it they had dinner at the Falls Café the other night."

"Yes, but after the dinner, they decided they were better off as friends. I'm not sure what happened, which is too bad."

Too bad because Margot liked boasting about her matchmaking success stories. So far, the Andrews siblings had been her biggest successes. Only Flynn remained single.

"I haven't heard that." Then again, Anna had seen few people since the wedding. Callie had taken time off from Wags and Tails, the doggy daycare she owned and where Anna worked as a groomer, to spend time with family in town for the holidays. Anna had happily worked additional hours for her friend and boss.

"Let's see what happens between them at midnight." Anna managed not to snort at her own joke, which should earn her a gold star. Flynn Andrews—make that Dr. Flynn

Andrews—didn't seem like the kind of guy to go without a New Year's kiss. And Pippa, the beautiful, willowy flower shop owner who loved the spotlight, was more of an ostentatious doctor's type than Anna, who preferred to remain in the background where no one noticed her.

"Pippa left with Timmy." Margot glanced over her shoulder. "Not sure if they're friends or more, but Flynn's here alone, and so are you."

"He doesn't like me." The words rushed out like too much dog shampoo when the spout broke at the shop.

Margot smiled mischievously. "He doesn't know you."

Anna took a step back. "I'd rather he didn't."

Margot tilted her head with a questioning expression. "Why's that, dear?"

Anna didn't want to have this conversation. She liked Margot, even if the woman was nosy and thought she was some sort of superhero matchmaker. "I know he's your nephew-in-law, but he's…"

"What?" Margot pressed.

Anna glanced around to make sure no one was nearby. She leaned closer to Margot to keep from having to talk too loud since Callie was also her best friend and boss. "He's cocky."

"Yes, but surgeons… Doctors, in general, are like that."

Margot didn't sound upset. That was good, but still, Anna shrugged. "Not my type."

"But he's so handsome."

She wasn't wrong. It pained Anna to admit how attractive Flynn was with thick dark hair, piercing amber-green eyes, and camera-ready features. But those things weren't enough to make her see beyond his sucky, stuck-up attitude. He didn't even try to hide the fact he didn't like Anna or Milo.

No, thank you. Especially since he appeared to be Margot's new matchmaking project. Anna stopped herself from shuddering. Besides, she wasn't convinced Pippa had moved on that easily. Timmy was younger than Pippa—not that age mattered. But he was still working his way through college while she owned a business on First Avenue. The two seemed more like friends than potential life partners. "Looks aren't everything."

"If you say so." Margot grabbed a puffed pastry appetizer from a platter. "But don't hide in the shadows. You've never been a wallflower, Anna Kent. So don't start now. Go have fun with or without Flynn."

"I will." Never argue with Margot was an unwritten rule in Silver Falls. One Anna wouldn't break.

Raine and Keaton approached holding hands. They were the definition of opposites but fit perfectly together.

Anna couldn't help but think of relationship goals when she looked at them. "How was your mini honeymoon?"

Raine leaned into Keaton's side. "Too short. I wish we could have stayed longer. But it was perfect and so romantic."

The look of contentment on Raine's face sent envy surging through Anna. It wasn't the first time that had happened tonight. It wouldn't be the last. She was truly happy for her friend—for all her friends—but Anna didn't know how she would fit in with the lovey-dovey couples who wanted to spend all their time together. Their treasured girls' nights might become the couples' date nights.

Anna swallowed around the lump in her throat. "Leavenworth at Christmastime is like visiting a holiday movie set."

She'd visited the German-themed town located west of Silver Falls a few times.

"It is." Keaton toyed with the ends of Raine's hair. "A film that takes place in Germany except everyone speaks English."

Raine shook her head. "He tried speaking German, and everyone thought he was a tourist visiting the States for the holidays."

"Wait. I thought you spoke Norwegian?" Anna asked Keaton.

"I do," he answered. "But I speak other languages, too."

"Remember, Callie calls him the brainy professor," Raine teased.

Callie had names like that for each of her three brothers. But Keaton's fit the best. In November, he'd been offered a job at Summit Ridge University. The new semester began next week. "Well, he is brainy and a professor so…"

Keaton bowed slightly. "Thanks, Anna."

"I'm glad you guys could get away," she added.

"Us, too." Keaton brushed his lips over Raine's head. "We'll take a real honeymoon during spring break or the summer, depending on when Raine can get away from Tea Leaves and Coffee Beans."

Raine giggled. "You really like saying the name of the coffee shop, don't you?"

He shrugged, nonchalantly. "I like the way it rolls off the tongue. And it is where we met."

Raine smiled at him, the heart eyes in full effect. "There's no rush. We have plenty of time to take a honeymoon and the rest of our lives for vacations."

If Raine wasn't such a great friend, Anna might gag. "You'll figure it out."

Keaton nodded. "Margot's been pushing for details."

"She wants to take credit for us getting married," Raine explained.

Anna laughed. "She's been gloating since you got engaged. Her feet didn't touch the ground on your wedding day."

"I'm okay with that." Raine glanced around as if looking for Silver Falls's favorite matchmaker. "But Flynn better watch his back. I think he's Margot's next target."

"No doubt." Anna lowered her voice. "She wants me to dance with him tonight. He and Pippa seemed so tight at your wedding, but Margot told me they decided to be just friends."

"Not surprising." Keaton picked up a mini-cheesecake bite. "My brother doesn't have time to sleep. All he does is work. Dating wouldn't appeal to him."

Raine nodded. "Pippa wants something serious. Timmy's going to help her set up a profile on a new dating app."

Mystery solved. And that made more sense than the two of them dating. "So that's why they left early."

Keaton laughed. "As Silver Falls turns. Everyone knows everyone's business. Or if they don't, they will tomorrow."

"Yes," Anna and Raine said in unison and then laughed.

Raine sipped eggnog from a glass on the table. "If Margot can't play matchmaker with Flynn, she'll set her sights on someone new."

"Someone like you, Anna," Keaton said.

"She gave up on me after Davis, but thanks for the warning." Anna eyed a bite-sized brownie. So tempting, but she'd eaten enough sweets. "I need to check on Milo. He's been quiet for too long, and that's never a good sign."

Anna wove her way through the crowd in the living room. Taryn and Garrett laughed with Callie and Brandt. Mrs. Jones straightened Mr. Jones's collar. The Hurleys held hands. One couple after another. Robin Baxter, who also worked for Raine and was recently divorced, had stayed home with her two kids. Now that Pippa had left the party, Anna and Margot appeared to be the only single women there.

Weird. Or perhaps, this was Anna's new normal, and she was destined to be a singleton her entire life. Her children would be fur babies, and she'd own a grooming salon someday.

Not a bad life.

Only not the one she'd dreamed about for so long.

Still, she didn't regret her past decisions. She could've gone out with Davis Tucker again, but that didn't mean they would have worked out when they wanted different things. Well, until he met the woman who became his new wife.

He'd quickly changed his mind about what he wanted then.

Don't think about him.

Anna hurried into the entryway. The music and conversations kept her from hearing any paw sounds or barks. The hallway doors were closed, and Margot would never lock the dogs in a room. They must be on the second floor.

She climbed the stairs.

Only one door was open. She peeked inside.

Milo, Rex, Autumn, Sadie, and Angus slept in the middle of a queen-sized bed. An adorable pile of pups. Two large, a medium sized, and two small ones.

Warmth flowed through Anna. She removed her phone from her pocket and snapped several photos to share with Callie, Raine, and Margot tomorrow.

"Hey," a man's voice called out.

She turned to face him.

Dr. Flynn Andrews, board-certified surgeon—as he liked to tell everyone—strode toward her. His hair bounced with each step. "Looking for the doctor in the house?"

His flirtatious tone was impossible to miss.

She fought the urge to roll her eyes. Anna might not like Flynn, but Callie, who was his sibling, and Taryn and Raine who were his in-laws, they were stuck with him. Anna needed to be civil. Since he lived in L.A., she wouldn't have to deal with him much so that was a plus.

Anna motioned into the guest bedroom. "Looks like you'll have company tonight."

A puzzled expression crossed Flynn's face. He peered around her.

And his jaw dropped. "What are those mutts doing on my bed? Especially your troublemaker."

Milo got into his fair share of trouble, no sense denying the obvious, but Anna loved him unconditionally. "It's Margot's guest bed. And the door wasn't shut. That's an open invitation to dogs used to being on furniture and having the run of a house."

He took a closer look and shrugged. "I guess they aren't hurting anything."

His stiff tone and posture were dead giveaways. "Not a dog lover?"

"We never had pets growing up. My dad's allergic, and my parents were too busy with work and us. Though Callie's Rex is cool, and Keaton's Autumn is sweet."

"You know, it's never too late to get your first pet."

"Not interested." Flynn bit his lip. "In dogs, that is. Now you…I've been looking for you."

He struck a casual pose against the doorframe that belonged in a high-fashion photo shoot.

"Why?" she asked.

"It's New Year's Eve." He leaned forward. "Did you come with a plus-one?"

She drew back. "No."

"Neither did I." He pointed at himself and then at her. "We're the only single people below the age of forty here—you know what that means?"

The expectant gleam in his eyes confused her. "What?"

He wagged his eyebrows. "You. Me. A kiss when the clock strikes midnight."

She stared at him in disbelief. The guy didn't want to kiss *her*. He didn't like her. Or Milo. It wasn't as if she liked him. The guy had bugged her the first time he stepped into Wags and Tails.

And then Anna remembered.

The Andrews brothers were a competitive lot. He must be after bragging rights or something. Most likely, he didn't want to be the only one who didn't get a kiss to start off the new year. But the idea of asking her…

Did he think she was desperate for a kiss because she didn't have a boyfriend and was an easy target?

Probably.

Her hands balled until her fingernails dug into her palms.

His mouth curved into a sexy grin. "Let's go downstairs for the countdown."

No doubt because he wanted his brothers to see him kiss a woman.

Unbelievable.

The arrogant surgeon was hot. But the guy knew he had looks and money and all the other things women were taught to value in a husband. What he didn't possess was a thoughtful or humble bone in his body.

"I'm a great kisser." Flynn pulled something rectangular from his pocket and held it out to her. "Breath mint?"

Even if she'd been tempted—a New Year's kiss had been on her list—she wasn't interested in kissing him.

"No, thanks." Anna stared down her nose. "I hope you have a plan B for midnight. Because I'd rather kiss Milo."

Chapter Two

O N NEW YEAR'S Day, Flynn sat on his sister and brother-in-law's living room couch fully awake. That shouldn't be an accomplishment at his age and at ten o'clock in the morning, but surprisingly, his eyes didn't automatically close. For the first time in months, he wasn't tired.

He relished in the moment of awake-ness.

This was good progress.

For the past few months, he'd fallen asleep the minute he sat anywhere. That had happened even after he arrived in Silver Falls.

Not unexpected with a surgeon in their practice on maternity leave and him picking up the slack. Thankfully, she'd returned to work the week before Keaton's wedding. That meant spending the holidays in Silver Falls, and Flynn wouldn't work as much when he went home. The closer he got to forty, the less he could function well on only a few hours of shut-eye.

Getting older sucked. But at least caffeine existed, and he sipped the best coffee he'd ever tasted, a delicious holiday blend, courtesy of Raine. Nothing like having sisters-in-law who owned a bakery and a tea and coffee shop. His brothers had married great wives. Taryn and Raine made Garrett and Keaton deliriously happy. Marriage wasn't on Flynn's radar. His job got in the way of relationships, so he just dated when he got the chance. Unfortunately, his schedule had limited his ability to date or do much outside of work.

He stretched out his legs.

College football played on the TV, but Flynn ignored the game. Concentrating on anything was difficult with every member of the Andrews and Winslow families talking over each other. Something they'd done at every other family holiday gathering, including the massive Monopoly marathon that made Callie cry, Garrett yell, and Keaton boast about winning. Even with the addition of Brandt and Taryn's families, some things never changed.

Callie came out from the kitchen. She wore a nutcracker sweater over a pair of leggings. His sister celebrated Christmas until Epiphany, so she had a few more days before she put away the holiday attire and accessories.

She sat next to him. "Please don't tell me you're still relying on caffeine to fuel yourself."

"First of the day." He raised his cup. "I'd say it's all I need except Raine outdid herself, so I might want a second. Emphasis on want, not need."

"Oh, the new blend. I haven't tried it. Brandt says it's his new favorite."

Flynn held out his cup to her. "Want a sip?"

"Not right now." Callie studied him. "Silver Falls must agree with you. You look more rested."

"Sleep agrees with me."

He glanced around the living room decked for Christmas with a tree and a mantel draped with garland. Mismatched snow people figurines and ornaments on the trees were the opposite of the designer-styled holiday décor at his parents' house in Beverly Hills, but Callie didn't need a matching color scheme or a themed tree. Her decorations were warm and homey and one hundred percent his little sister.

"You've done well for yourself here, baby sis." He sipped his coffee.

Her face flushed. "Are you ever going to stop calling me that?"

"Nope, baby sis." Her eye-roll didn't bother Flynn. "That's what you'll always be to me, and I'm so proud of you. You've created a home and become a part of the community."

She beamed. "Thanks. I..." As Callie sucked in a breath, her face paled. She clutched the couch.

Flynn placed his cup on the coffee table, grabbed her hand, and felt her pulse. Not too fast. "What hurts?"

She closed her eyes for a moment and then shook her hand free. "Nothing. I didn't get enough sleep last night."

Maybe. Her eyes weren't bloodshot. He touched her forehead: not warm. Her skin wasn't clammy. "Did you go in for your annual physical?"

"Yes, Dr. Flynn. You're as bad as Mom."

"Let's call Mom over here."

"No." The word shot from Callie's mouth. She leaned closer. "I'm guessing you haven't had a physical yourself in a long time, even though Mom told you to make an appointment when you were so tired before Thanksgiving."

Callie wasn't wrong, but he didn't have time. "I see doctors every day."

She shot him one of Mom's I'm-the-chief-of-staff-don't-mess-with-me looks. "Not the same thing."

No, it wasn't. But this trip had shown Flynn the best medicine was a vacation where he could sleep uninterrupted. He'd done that at Margot's, away from the three sets of happy newlyweds, while his parents and Brandt's folks stayed at a pet-free vacation rental where dog allergies wouldn't be an issue.

"We're not talking about me," Flynn reminded her.

"Then we're both good."

He didn't know whether to believe her, but he would watch her and ask Mom if she'd noticed anything off with Callie. "We are."

"Though I still think Silver Falls agrees with you," Callie said with a soft smile.

Flynn loved what L.A. offered, but he'd needed to get away from work. He'd lost count of the times he'd been too tired to drive home or fallen asleep in the break room. Being well rested gave him a new outlook. A happier one.

"Our family's all here, and I'm not on call," he admitted. "That's a win-win."

"And why you no longer look like an extra in a zombie movie."

"Such a compliment." In all honesty, zombies looked better than he had before Keaton's wedding. As soon as Flynn had arrived, Margot fed him, took away his phone, given him a glass of warm milk, and put him to bed. He must've slept sixteen hours that first day. "But Silver Falls is my go-to place when I want to sleep."

Callie smirked. "Shouldn't that be your bedroom?"

"Ha-ha."

"I'm not kidding. But it's nice to see you not yawning all the time or needing us to explain everything to you."

"That happened once." When Keaton had decided to return to Silver Falls in November. And in Flynn's defense, many people mixed up Washington State and Washington D.C.

"I'd say more than once, but you're back to being the old Flynn." Callie leaned into him. "That's all that matters."

He hugged her. "I was still your big brother, albeit a tired one."

Mischief gleamed in her eyes. "You're in town for a few more days. Why don't you give Pippa a call?"

Flynn should have known. He swallowed a sigh. "Margot's matchmaking is rubbing off on you."

"You and Pippa—"

"Had fun dancing at Keaton and Raine's reception. When it was just the two of us, we realized we wanted different things."

"You mean she wants a relationship, and you want—"

"Not that. My life's in L.A. Her flower shop is here."

"Garrett and Keaton—"

"Aren't me." Flynn didn't like the way Callie's face fell. "I'm thrilled you love Silver Falls, but a small town isn't me. I'll visit as much as I can. I promise."

She bit her lip.

"Have I ever broken a promise to you?" he asked, knowing the answer.

"No, but a girl can hope to have her family living in the same place."

"Mom and Dad aren't planning to move."

"Maybe after they retire, but I was thinking of my brothers."

"You have two out of three." Flynn kissed her forehead. "That's more than you imagined would be here with you."

She tilted her chin slightly. "True. And you never know what might happen in the future."

"With Mom and Dad, yes. But I'm a big-city, trauma-level-one kind of guy. And I'm sure there's a city-loving woman walking around in stilettos carrying a designer briefcase who'll not only be perfect for me but also able to put up with me."

Callie shook her head. "You're no fun."

"I'm a lot of fun." When he wasn't at work or exhausted or relaxing with his family.

"I just hope your said perfect woman isn't working on a holiday. The two of you would never see each other."

She had a point, but Mom and Dad's marriage had survived two high-powered careers. Sure, there'd been some rocky times Callie was too young to remember, but his parents would celebrate their forty-year wedding anniversary in three months.

Ding-dong.

Flynn glanced around. Everyone in the family was there.

"Who's that?"

Callie grinned. "You'll see."

"If it's Pippa—"

"Not Pippa. I wouldn't put a dear friend in an awkward position."

"Only your brother."

Callie ignored him.

Brandt opened the door. "Hey…"

A ball of white bolted into the living room and made a beeline for the kitchen. If Milo was there, that meant…

"Anna." Brandt motioned the dog groomer inside. "Come in. We've been expecting you."

Flynn shot a sideward glance at his sister. "Isn't this a family gathering?"

Callie's lips narrowed. "Anna and Milo are family."

Fine. Enough people were there he wouldn't have to talk to the dog groomer who'd turned down his midnight kiss. It wasn't as if he'd wanted to kiss her. He'd just wanted to kiss someone, and Anna had been alone at the party, so why not?

It was only a kiss, which was why he'd given Margot a peck last night as the clock struck twelve. Margot had made him promise to make it short and no tongue. He'd promised and crossed his heart, something he hadn't done in over thirty years. Brandt's aunt cracked him up.

Callie grinned at her employee. "So happy you could make it."

Anna held a bag in her hand and waved. "I brought the artichoke spinach dip you love."

"Thanks," Callie said. "Put it on the table. I'll be there in a minute."

"Better be careful," Flynn whispered. "Anna probably let her menace of a dog lick the dip."

Milo had ruined Callie's Christmas window a little over a year ago. That wasn't the only time he'd caused problems, yet Anna acted as if he was the best dog ever. She spoiled the mutt instead of teaching him to behave. And if she wanted to kiss a dog instead of Flynn…

Blech.

Callie elbowed him. "Stop it. You look like you bit into a lemon. Milo is spirited. And wait until you try the dip. It's homemade. And so good. Stop acting like you're nine and want a can to spray the cooties away."

"Cooties?"

"That's what you guys used to say girls had."

"A long time ago."

"You're not acting like it was that long ago." Callie stood. "Be nice to my best friend."

"An employee shouldn't be your best friend."

She gave him the stink eye.

He pasted on his bedside-manner smile, but that was as much as his sister would get out of him where Anna Kent was involved. "Always nice."

Callie shook her head and hurried over to Anna.

Flynn *was* nice, but that didn't mean he wanted to try the dip or befriend Anna. The woman and her dog rubbed him the wrong way. Anna had been good friends with Nick and Robin Baxter, the same Nick who tried to ruin Callie's wedding and Raine's bakery. He also worried about Anna taking advantage of Callie. The dog groomer acted more like a partner than an employee.

Given Anna didn't glance Flynn's way suggested she knew he was on to her and wanted to keep her distance. He would see if Garrett could use one of the law firm's investigators to run a background check on Anna. Something about her was sketchy.

A few minutes later, Brandt and Callie stood in front of the fireplace. The two made a striking couple, and it was clear to see how in love they were even though Flynn and the rest of the family hadn't been so sure about the life Callie had built for herself so far away from home.

Brandt cleared his throat. "If we could have everyone's attention, please. This won't take long, and then we can eat and watch football."

"Or play Monopoly so I can win again," Keaton shouted.

Garrett tsked. "No heckling from the crowd, Professor."

Callie shot Flynn a glance as if daring him to say something, but he saw no reason to play those games. He picked up his coffee and sipped.

Everyone quieted. A first for the Andrews family. Flynn was still getting to know the families of his new in-laws—the Winslows and Lawsons.

Milo barked.

Anna shushed him.

Flynn wouldn't be surprised if the dog made a flying leap onto the table and gobbled up everything in snout's reach.

Brandt quieted people. "Thank you for joining us today after we kicked off the new year in style last night at Aunt

Margot's house. We thought this would be the perfect time to make an announcement."

Callie held up a small white piece of paper. "In October at a girls' night, we had Chinese takeout. Pippa, Taryn, Anna, and I all received the same fortune that said, 'Prepare for expansion.'"

"I remember that," Taryn said. "I expanded the bakery's menu."

Anna nodded. "Wags and Tails added boarding."

Callie and Brandt shared a look. "That's what I thought it meant. Turns out…"

"We're pregnant," Brandt shouted.

Margot jumped up and down. "I'm going to be a great-aunt!"

Flynn's mouth gaped. Pregnant? Callie?

Mom and Dad ran to the happy couple. Brandt's parents followed them. Lots of hugs and happy tears and high fives.

Rex and Autumn watched from the sidelines. Milo barked and ran around like he wanted to be the center of attention.

Anna wiped her eyes, but Flynn couldn't tell if she was faking the tears or not. He would give her the benefit of the doubt. Maybe she was worried if a baby would change Callie's commitment to the doggy daycare.

Brandt's hand settled on Callie's stomach with an almost reverent touch.

Garrett clapped Flynn's shoulders. "We're going to be uncles."

"Our baby sis is going to be a mom." Flynn shook his

head. "We need to set up a trust fund for the baby."

"I know someone who can help with that."

Of course as a top trial attorney Garrett would. Flynn motioned to Keaton who bent over to speak to Callie's stomach. "We'll leave the education decisions up to the professor, but we'll fund the best schools."

Garrett nodded. "Glad I live in Silver Falls."

"You're still a partner in your L.A. law firm. You just have a satellite office here."

"Not going back." Garrett's gaze drifted from Callie to Taryn. "Especially now that I'll have a niece or nephew in town."

Flynn understood. "It's not a long flight."

But trips depended on his work schedule, which he would have to keep under control so he didn't end up hating life and sleep-deprived again.

Garrett nudged him. "The parents are off to take care of the food. It's our turn."

Flynn followed Garrett over to Callie and Brandt. Keaton was right behind them.

She hugged each of her brothers. "No spoiling your niece or nephew, or we'll set limits."

"Don't worry about us." Keaton motioned to Margot, who stared at her phone. "I think she's already ordering baby stuff to outfit a nursery at her house."

"There goes my guest bedroom," Flynn announced dramatically.

"She has three guest bedrooms," Garrett explained. "I'm sure your room is safe."

Flynn focused on Callie. "How are you feeling?"

"I've had some light-headedness and morning sickness, but otherwise, I'm good. Nothing's been bad. Midmorning to lunchtime is usually when it hits the worst. Anna had no idea about the baby. She's been covering for me but—"

"Anna won't mind continuing that until you feel better," Brandt said.

Callie nodded.

That wasn't enough for Flynn. Callie's pregnancy explained her dizziness earlier, if that was all the symptoms were. "Be sure to tell your OB what happened on the couch."

"What happened?" Brandt, Garrett, and Keaton asked in unison.

"I was a little light-headed. It was nothing," Callie explained.

Her answer satisfied no one, including Flynn. He looked at Brandt, who nodded.

"I'll make sure she mentions it," Brandt said. "And I'm glad all three of you are here. We've been discussing who the godparents will be."

Callie nodded. "Since Garrett and Keaton live here, we want Flynn to be the godfather. That'll give him another reason to come to Silver Falls."

Pride shot through Flynn. He stood taller.

Margot came up like a hurricane about to make landfall. Her face beamed brighter than a solar flare. "Who's going to be the godmother?"

Callie peered around them. "Anna. She's my best

friend."

Margot clapped her hands. "Perfect choice. And you know what this means."

Everyone stared at Anna.

"What?" Callie asked.

"Anna and Flynn need to host the baby shower," Margot announced. "Of course, we'll all lend a hand."

Keaton snorted. "Flynn arrange a baby shower. That's a good one."

"As if you'd do better," Flynn countered.

Keaton's chest puffed. "As a matter of fact, I would. The Boo Bash I helped Raine organize received rave reviews."

"Brothers," Callie muttered under her breath.

Flynn wouldn't disappoint Callie and Brandt. "No worries. I'll figure it out."

How hard could hosting a baby shower be?

Not even worth a second thought. Flynn had this. He would be the best godfather anyone in Silver Falls or the state of Washington had ever seen. People would talk about what he did for his niece or nephew for years, even decades, to come.

"I'm honored," he admitted.

Garrett rolled his eyes. "Well, when he gets overwhelmed or can't keep up, Keaton and I will take over."

Flynn stepped in front of the other two. "I've got this."

Margot's blue eyes twinkled. "Don't forget about Anna."

"What about me?" Anna walked up, holding a fruit kabob over a napkin.

"We want you to be the baby's godmother," Callie said.

"If you want to be."

"I do. I'm so happy you asked." Anna one-arm hugged Callie and then Brandt. "I'll get working on the baby shower right away. Coed, right?"

Wait. Flynn scratched his head. How did Anna know about this stuff?

"Yes, please." Callie smiled at Anna. "Oh, and Flynn's the godfather, so he'll help you."

And there was the catch. Flynn should have known. He would bet Anna had only been playing hard to get last night. Face it. The woman wanted to date and kiss him. Her rejection had to be a ploy. She must have figured out Callie was pregnant. He was, after all, the only pick for a godfather.

Anna eyed him as if selecting what type of meat to buy at the butcher counter. "Flynn, huh?"

For some reason, she sounded amused, and he didn't like it. "Yes, me. And I can help with the shower."

Especially if that was one of his responsibilities as Margot had implied.

"Let's discuss it after we eat," Anna suggested.

Flynn had a better idea. "Or we do it tomorrow when it's not a holiday."

If he kept pushing off the discussion, he might not have to deal with Anna until he was in L.A. The farther Flynn stayed away from her and Milo, the better.

Chapter Three

O N TUESDAY MORNING, Anna glanced at the calendar—a gift from Mrs. Sellwood, a customer—hung behind the doggy daycare's checkout counter. As Anna grabbed a pen and crossed out the first two days of the month, unease slithered through her. It was early January, but springtime would arrive soon. That was when Callie and Brandt wanted to have the baby shower.

If the growing knot in Anna's stomach were a dog bone, it would be big enough for a mastiff. The third of January meant Flynn Andrews left town tomorrow. He hadn't wanted to discuss the baby shower on the first. The texts Anna sent yesterday remained unanswered. That meant the "arrogant surgeon" was ghosting her.

She groaned.

Milo and Rex who lay next to each other on the dog pillow by the counter both raised their heads.

"Sorry, boys. Didn't mean to disturb your nap." Passing on her aggravation to the dogs or clients would let Flynn win. She wasn't as competitive as the males in the Andrews family, but she would make sure Callie came out on top with the baby shower. "Go back to sleep. It'll be okay."

And it would be.

Once she figured out Flynn's issue with the baby shower or with her. Something told Anna it was most likely her since he adored his younger sister. Which meant he had some questions to answer.

Well, once she tracked him down.

Callie and Brandt's baby shower would be perfect in every way. Yes, Anna and Flynn could have picked a date and made all the plans these past two days, but he was still in Silver Falls. She might not be a highly revered surgeon, but even a dog groomer understood pinning him down to discuss the party would be harder, if not impossible, once he left town.

All she had to do was find Flynn.

Anna would. She hadn't asked Margot for help yet—that was her last choice—but others had been on Flynn watch since yesterday. So far, no sightings, but it wasn't even eight o'clock in the morning. Both Sam and Mary Jo were with the dogs, so Anna could run out for a few minutes.

A perfect plan.

Once Dr. Flynn Andrews turned up.

Dogs barked from the playroom.

Rex and Milo sat, ears perked. Both stared at her.

"Want to go back there and play with the others?"

Milo jumped off the pillow. He didn't need more of an invitation than that. Rex lumbered slowly, his older legs needing time to warm up.

She smiled at the two best dog buds. "You know where to go."

As Rex picked up the pace, Anna followed them to the doorway.

"Incoming," she yelled to the back.

"I see 'em." Sam and Mary Jo would make sure all the dogs—no matter shape, size, or age—had fun. Becca wouldn't be in until school got out. Kelly and Frasier worked the overnight shifts for the boarding guests. That reminded Anna...

She returned to the counter and checked to see if anyone was missing today. Nope. Everyone was there. That would give her time to restock—

Buzz.

The front of her apron vibrated. She pulled her phone from the pocket to see a text from Robin Baxter.

Robin: *Flynn's here with Brecken.*

Yes! This was Anna's chance. She wasn't a stalker, but she wasn't above an ambush for Callie's sake. If he even slightly cared about his sister's feelings, this wouldn't be necessary. Pippa hadn't said much about the guy other than she wanted more than a holiday romance, which was why they'd decided to be just friends. That information confirmed what Anna had thought. Flynn cared only about himself.

She leaned through the doorway again. "Everyone's checked in. I'm going to Tea Leaves and Coffee Beans. I'll bring back the usual."

Sam peeked around the corner. "Get a peppermint tea for Callie. That helped my mom when she was pregnant. We can keep it in the fridge in case Callie comes in and heat it up in the microwave."

"Great idea." Anna smiled at Sam, who attended Summit Ridge University. "You're going to be a fabulous RN."

"If I get into the program. Spots are limited. I heard the competition is tough." He didn't sound confident.

"You're doing everything you can to be accepted." Brandt had arranged for Sam to receive the same scholarship the older kids of his now defunct company's employees received. "And if you don't, it means you're meant to try a new school or do something different, like be a vet."

His jaw dropped. "Getting into veterinary school is even harder than the nursing program."

"Harder doesn't mean impossible." Words she needed to remember about her current single status. She'd overcome worse circumstances, which not even her closest friends knew about. Moving to Silver Falls had been the fresh start she'd desperately needed. "Be back in a few minutes. And I won't forget the peppermint tea."

No one expected Callie to come in until after lunch if at all. She'd made it in yesterday right before closing, but her complexion had been a tad green, so she'd picked up some things to do at home and left. It wasn't a problem. Anna and the rest of the staff could handle the doggy daycare. The most important thing was Callie's health and the baby's well-being.

Anna grabbed her purse and her coat. She didn't bother with a hat and gloves. The coffee shop was just down the street.

A few steps out the door, the crisp temperature brought

goose bumps. Each exhalation of her breath hung on the air in a small puff. She shoved her bare hands into her jacket pockets. Gloves would have been smart. So would have her hat.

The cold temperature might explain why few people were out on First Avenue. She quickened her pace, reached the door to Tea Leaves and Coffee Beans in record time, and rushed inside.

Robin stood behind the counter at the espresso machine. "Hey. You got here quickly."

"Today, I'm more hare than tortoise." Anna scanned the seating area. Familiar faces sat at tables, but only a few were filled. "Can I get the usual, except sub a peppermint tea for Callie's drink?"

"Sure thing." Robin tilted her head toward the sitting area. "He's got his back to you. Sitting with Brecken."

Anna took another look over her shoulder and saw Flynn. She paid for the order and tucked two dollars in the tip jar. "Thanks."

From the back, Flynn's hair appeared thick and styled, the kind that looked good from any angle. Brecken spoke animatedly. The teenager, a freshman at the community college, worked at Lawson's Bakery.

"Are you kidding me, man?" Brecken took an envelope from Flynn and smiled big. "Appreciate your vote of confidence. I'll let you know how this quarter goes."

"You'd better."

Brecken pushed back from the table, grabbed his backpack from an empty chair, and stood. "Thanks again, Doc.

You're the best."

Anna wouldn't go that far, but whatever Flynn had given the young man seemed to have gone over well. Callie had mentioned Brecken had a special relationship with Flynn and Keaton, but Anna knew nothing more than that. Surprising given Silver Falls wasn't a place for keeping secrets.

As Brecken headed to the door, Anna went up to Flynn. "Got a minute?"

Flynn glanced at his phone on the table. "I have five."

"I won't waste any time then." She sat. "We need to pick a date for the baby shower."

Lines creased Flynn's forehead. He stared as if her skin had turned purple and she'd grown horns. "The shower's months away."

"Yes, but I found the cutest save-the-date email cards. Callie and Brandt want all their friends and family to be there, so I thought giving advance notice would be smart."

Flynn sipped his coffee and then wiped his mouth with a napkin. "Isn't that a little excessive for a baby shower?"

"This is the first child of the Andrews family's next generation. Excessive should be the adjective for the event, right?" She kept her voice lighthearted.

"Callie did seem excited about the shower."

Okay, that was progress. "They don't want to know if the baby's a boy or a girl, so I was thinking we could go with a rainbow color scheme."

"Rainbow?" He rubbed his neck. "What about black and gold?"

She nearly laughed until she saw the serious gleam in his

eyes. "How many baby showers have you attended?"

He tilted his head as if counting them. "Zero."

O-kay. Except it wasn't. "I don't think Callie wants a fancy baby shower like her wedding."

"You said excessive."

"Excessive as in over-the-top with cute and cuddly things."

His confusion might have been adorable if he weren't such a jerk. "Things such as...?"

"Rainbows, unicorns, and stuffies." He appeared totally befuddled. Maybe only pediatricians learned about babies, and other doctors picked up knowledge as needed. The only things she knew about med school came from watching *Grey's Anatomy*. "Stuffed animals," she clarified.

"Oh."

"Do you have any dates in mind?" she asked when he didn't say anything.

"I'll have to check my schedule. See when I'm on call."

"The only weekend that won't work is the last weekend in March. That's when the annual Spring Fling is held."

"Let me guess. The Spring Fling is an event the First Avenue Business Association puts on."

"Ding. Ding. Ding. The doctor got it right."

"Well, we wouldn't want to overlap with an event like that."

"No, we wouldn't." See, they agreed. No reason they couldn't work together. "Please let me know what other days—"

"We should hire an event planner."

Anna's shoulders dropped. She reminded herself he was a surgeon who probably lived in Beverly Hills like his doctor mother and lawyer father did. His upbringing and worldview were nothing like hers. Crack houses and foster care were the antithesis of everything he knew.

She counted backward from ten to keep herself calm. Getting upset wouldn't help the situation. "Callie and Brandt expect us to do it. I don't want to disappoint them."

"As long as they get a baby shower, they won't complain."

"Callie wouldn't ever complain, but she'd be disappointed if we handed something as special as her and Brandt's baby shower to a stranger. Who knows if the event planner would want Lawson's Bakery to make the desserts or have Pippa do some centerpieces? And…"

He leaned forward. "What?"

"We're the baby's godparents." Anna needed to be upfront about this even if it affected her working with Flynn. Her heart told her she was right, and he was wrong. "Is this how we want to start off our relationship with the kid? Spending money instead of giving time and putting in effort."

Flynn glanced at his phone. "That's a bit extreme."

"Maybe, but I wouldn't feel right hiring someone. Not to mention, I don't have that kind of money."

"I don't mind paying—"

"I mind." Fine, she would say what they both knew. "Look, it's clear you don't like me."

"I never said that." The words came quickly.

"Am I wrong?"

Flynn didn't answer.

"I don't mean to put you on the spot," Anna continued, even though she'd done that. "But being godparents means we'll be invited to all the kid's milestone events and birthdays. I don't know about you since you're not from Silver Falls, but I plan to be at all the things."

"Me, too."

Anna was afraid of that. Her muscles tightened. "If we're not civil to each other, people will notice."

"Most people only see what they want to see."

"Over time, they'll see more. Neither of us have poker faces."

His lips curved upward with a hint of a smile. "You sure don't."

Neither did he, but Anna wanted to be the bigger person. Face it, she had more at stake. Might as well just say that, too. "Planning the baby shower is the first thing we've been asked to do as godparents. If we can't do that together, what will it mean going forward? I don't want to give Callie and Brandt a reason to regret who they chose."

"They wouldn't."

"But if they did…" The empty space in Anna's heart grew larger. "You're family. I'm the one who'd be out if it came to that. Tell me what I did to make you hate me, so I can fix it."

"I don't hate you."

"Dislike then."

"We can go with that."

She knew she was right. "So…"

"It's not one thing."

She nearly laughed, more out of nervousness. Nothing about this was funny. "Just a general dislike for unknown reasons?"

He laughed. Of course, he did. The rich, deep sound rumbled in a much too pleasant way given the way he felt about her.

"When put that way, it sounds silly," he admitted. "But if you must know, I don't like your dog."

She understood that. "Milo isn't for everyone."

"I also don't like that you're friends with Nick and Robin Baxter."

"You might want to lower your voice because Robin is working behind the counter."

His head jerked around. "When did that happen?"

"In the fall. She and Nick are getting a divorce. Robin needed a job. Callie's friends with Robin. So is Taryn."

The lines on Flynn's face deepened. "But Nick—"

"Doesn't come around much. They sold their house." Anna didn't need to defend herself, but Flynn should know the truth. "I wasn't the only one who was friends with Nick. Callie, Taryn, and Raine were too, so if you're going to hold it against me…"

"You're untraceable."

She stiffened. "Excuse me?"

"I had a background check run on you. It's as if you didn't exist before you attended grooming school."

Unbelievable. Anna slumped in her chair. "You're as

overprotective as Callie said."

"Am I wrong?"

Every nerve ending went on alert. "My past has nothing to do with who I am today or putting on your sister and brother-in-law's baby shower."

A vein throbbed at his jawline. He seemed to think her past did matter.

Stalemate.

"I'm not a scammer if that's what you're worried about." Her gaze locked on his intense eyes. The gold glowed as if enflamed. "If I was a con artist, I would've picked a more lucrative field than animal grooming."

He sipped his coffee, but his gaze remained locked on her as if she were a tumor he wanted to cut out of his sister's life.

Time for damage control. All Anna had was her job and friendships in Silver Falls. Oh, and her fur babies. She didn't want to have to start over again, somewhere else. This was where she wanted to stay.

Forever.

No one, especially the arrogant surgeon, would mess things up for her.

She swallowed. "We should put on Callie's baby shower. If that's too much for you with your job and living in L.A., I understand. Just give me the dates that work, and we'll call it good."

As his brows drew together, he eyed her warily. "You'll do everything yourself?"

"I'm sure some of Callie's friends will pitch in, but yes,

I'll handle everything myself." Anna swallowed the lump in her throat that was bigger than the balance in her ever-dwindling checking account. One of her cats, Snowy, had needed teeth pulled. The vet cost way more than Anna had planned on spending for vet bills and depleted her savings account.

But desperate times called for desperate measures.

Cutting back on the prescription diet her babies ate wasn't an option, but she knew how to eat for only a few dollars a day. It wasn't the healthiest of diets, but a year or so of eating cheaply wouldn't kill her.

She raised her chin. "I'll pay for everything, too. I promise the baby shower will be perfect. Better than what any event planner would do."

Because she loved Callie and Brandt and their baby. Anna would do whatever it took for the shower to be what they wanted. Flynn might trust a stranger to do that, but Anna didn't. And this might get him to forget about her past.

A win-win.

He opened his mouth as if to say something but then pressed his lips together.

"Anna," Robin called out. "Your order is ready."

Flynn flinched.

"I need to go." Anna straightened. "What do you say? Do we have a deal?"

Chapter Four

THE NEXT DAY, Flynn placed his folded gray sweater into his suitcase sitting open on a luggage rack. Margot had her guest room set up like a hotel. He wanted for nothing. Probably why he felt so rested after being there for more than two weeks.

Only the ugly Christmas sweater hanging in the closet needed to be packed. He'd been forced to wear the eyesore for the family's annual holiday photo. This year, the Winslows and Lawsons had been officially added. And Raine, who had no other family, too. They'd all looked ridiculous in the sweaters, but Callie's smile had been North Star bright, making the humiliation worthwhile.

But the sweater would not go home with him.

Callie would likely want a repeat next year, so he would ask if she or Margot would keep the monstrosity for him. Most likely, all future holidays would be spent in Silver Falls. Last night over dinner, his die-hard L.A. parents mentioned buying a second home in Silver Falls. It appeared the arrival of a grandchild might change their retirement plans.

A niece or nephew, however, wasn't reason enough for Flynn to move to Silver Falls. He'd enjoyed his three stays with Margot. Her house felt more like a second home during this visit. But he was ready to work. Only this time, he would be smarter and not let himself get so worn out. As Callie had said on New Year's Day, the old Flynn was back. The constant yawning and confusion from being sleep-deprived were things of the past. He was ready to seize the day, make a difference for his patients, and live his best life. He'd accomplished the middle one, even while exhausted, but the other two not so much.

Flynn double-checked he hadn't left anything in the dresser drawers.

A knock sounded.

He straightened. "Come in."

Callie entered. Her face was drawn and pale.

Flynn patted the bed. "Sit. You look tired."

"I am." She plopped onto the mattress. "And fed up."

"Have you eaten today?"

She raised her hand as if to stop him from talking. "My OB says this is normal and not to be concerned. My morning sickness isn't why I'm here."

He sat next to her. "You want to spend some quality time with your favorite older brother before he leaves?"

"Not that either."

He acted as if she'd stabbed him in the heart. "You wound me."

"You deserve it." Her voice sharpened. "I can't believe you, Flynn Andrews."

The use of both names only happened when one of them was in trouble. He held up his hand in a mock surrender. "I didn't do it."

"You've never lied to me as far as I know. Don't start now."

He tried to think what might have happened between last night's dinner at Taryn and Garrett's house and now. Flynn came up blank. "I don't know what you're talking about."

"You're letting Anna organize and pay for the baby shower all by herself."

Oh, that. Flynn blew out a breath. He'd forgotten about the baby shower since Anna stepped up. The fact Callie knew proved the groomer was as much of a troublemaker as her little dog. "I didn't think Anna would run straight to you that fast."

The hurt in Callie's eyes reminded him of when she was a little girl and wanted him to make whatever was wrong better.

"So, it's true?" She sounded heartbroken. "You made a deal with Anna?"

Wait. Flynn straightened. Callie asked as if she wasn't certain about what happened. "Anna must've told you—"

"She didn't say anything to me. Three people who overheard you talking at the coffee shop called me." Callie rubbed her face. "They told me you're dumping the baby shower on my best friend, who you also accused of being a scammer."

His shoulders tightened. He hated seeing Callie so upset, and he wanted to have words with whoever had called her. She was too emotional. That stress wasn't good for her or the baby.

Flynn needed to keep calm. He took a breath to gather himself. "First, my conversation with Anna was private. People had no right to eavesdrop."

Callie's eyes flared. "Oh no you don't."

He flinched. This in-his-face Callie wasn't the baby sister he remembered. "Don't what?"

"You don't get to play the victim." She held up her hand and counted off on her fingers. "You agreed to let Anna put on a shower. You agreed to let her pay for everything, even though you probably earn her yearly salary in a month or two. You questioned her integrity. How dare you?"

He didn't understand her indignation. "I'm looking out for you, sis. I've been worried about you working so closely with Anna since I met her more than a year ago."

Callie's eyes darkened. "Why?"

"Something about her rubbed me the wrong way."

She scoffed. "You mean Anna didn't bow down and worship at your feet like most women."

It wasn't a question. Good, because he wouldn't lower himself to answer that. "Anna's reaction to me has nothing to do with this. Her bubbliness has to be fake. You might not be able to see it, but I do. Garrett gave me the name of someone his firm uses. I hired them to run a background check on your dog groomer. Did you know she's not on any social media? There's no digital footprint of her until she went to grooming school. It's like she appeared out of nowhere. That's not normal."

"Anna's worked at Wags and Tails longer than I have.

She was hired by the former owner and helped me so much when I purchased the business. If she wanted to steal from me or hurt me, she would have already done it."

"You don't know that."

"I do. Because she's my best friend. She rescues animals for a hobby. I can't even keep track of the cats she fosters so they can be adopted into forever homes."

Callie made Anna sound like some patron saint of animals or something. No one was that nice. "Her dog—"

"Milo isn't her evil minion." Callie shook her head. "Anna adopted him after he was rescued from a puppy mill. He was malnourished and possibly abused. He's come a long way."

Flynn wasn't a dog person, but he'd seen reports about puppy mills on the news. "I didn't know."

"You just assumed. The same as when you and everyone else thought I belonged in Beverly Hills not Silver Falls. Or if someone's life isn't available for full view in an internet search they must have something to hide, when maybe they have a compelling reason for not wanting to be found." Callie's voice softened. "Not everyone grew up safe and secure with loving parents like we did. There are valid reasons people don't want to be on social media or keep themselves untraceable. But whatever the reason, wanting privacy is enough."

Was Anna trying to keep herself safe or was she hiding? Flynn's mind went in a million different directions, none of them good. "Is Anna—"

"Not my story to tell, so don't ask."

He leaned back, trying to take it all in. "I didn't know there might be more—"

"You don't know her at all."

That much was true.

"And none of this excuses you for dumping the baby shower on Anna." Callie's tone was harsh.

"I offered to hire an event planner, but Anna felt we should do it ourselves."

"Because she knows that's what I would want."

"A planner—"

"Would put on a perfectly nice and probably elegant soiree. That's not me or Brandt. We want friends and fun."

"And rainbows."

"I love rainbows."

Of course, she did. "I—"

Callie held up her hand. "You weren't my first choice for godfather."

Her words slapped into him. "What?"

"I'm not saying this to be cruel, but you're a workaholic. You're either too busy or too exhausted. You make up for it by being generous with your money. I have no doubt you'll buy the baby the best presents and set up a college fund for him or her."

His face heated. He'd sent an email to Garrett's financial planner yesterday.

"I would prefer the baby to have godparents who are part of their life. But I don't expect to see you outside of major holidays, and that's only if you can get away."

Flynn wanted to disagree, but he couldn't. He only saw

Mom as much as he did because they worked at the same hospital. Otherwise, he visited his parents during the holidays or if something big happened like when Keaton lost his job in September.

"If you felt that way, why did you ask me?" Flynn asked.

"Brandt."

The name reverberated through Flynn. "Your husband wants me to be the godfather?"

She nodded. "He wants you to feel more included since you don't live in Silver Falls. He also thought the label might guilt you into coming back more often after the baby is born."

"Brandt's a smart man."

"Yes, he married me."

Flynn probably shouldn't ask, but he wanted to know. "Who did you want to be the baby's godfather?"

"Sam Merrill."

Flynn's jaw dropped. "The kid who works for you at Wags and Tails? He's so young and couldn't afford to buy the baby much."

"He's young, yes. But being a godparent isn't about money. Sam's hardworking and caring. But I agree with Brandt that you made the most sense."

Flynn didn't like her use of past tense. "I want to be the baby's godfather."

"Then you'll need to abide by some rules."

Or you'll be replaced was left unspoken but implied.

"What rules?" he asked.

"Your job requires a lot from you, so I don't expect you

in Silver Falls until the baby shower. But you can't leave Anna to do everything and pay for it on her own. That isn't fair."

"I'll work with her and pay." He wouldn't miss the money, so that would be easy to do and make Callie happy.

"Nothing about Anna is sketchy. This protective older brother routine of yours must stop. I love you, but I'm not a baby. I'm a wife." Callie touched her stomach. "And soon-to-be mother. Get off your high horse and apologize to Anna."

Or else.

Callie didn't have to say the words. They were written in bold, capital letters on her face.

Flynn was on shaky ground. "I will."

"You better. And be nice to her. The two of you need to get along." Callie's tone remained firm. "I can't afford to lose Anna. She's working so many extra hours right now. She did the same thing when Brandt and I went on our honeymoon. I'll need her to do that again when I take my maternity leave. If you do anything to make her quit, you'll be coming up here to help me with Wags and Tails. Got it?"

He shouldn't laugh when Callie was trying to be all serious, but he cracked a smile. "You sound like Mom right now."

Callie raised her chin. "Be glad I haven't told Mom what you did. Though I always could."

The words floated in the air between them.

"No need." He didn't need Mom involved. "I'll stop by Wags and Tails on my way to the airport."

Funny how Anna thought she would be the one kicked to the curb if something went wrong between them. Instead Flynn got the feeling he was the replaceable one. He'd never sensed that before. And he didn't like it. Not at all.

As FLYNN STEPPED through the door of Wags and Tails, a bell jingled. He stood in line behind an older woman at the counter with a small dog in her arms. The dog peered around and snarled at Flynn.

Why did some dogs hate him on sight?

The woman readjusted the dog so it could no longer see Flynn. "You're almost out of these organic dog treats. Better make sure Callie orders them."

Sam nodded. "She has, Mrs. Sellwood. They'll be on the shelf as soon as they arrive."

"Good. These are the only bones Madden can eat. The others give him the runs. Such a mess to clean up."

"I'm sure." Sam handed Mrs. Sellwood a small brown paper bag. "I'm happy these work for him and you. Have a nice day."

The guy seemed nice enough, but Flynn would be a better godfather to Callie and Brandt's baby.

Mrs. Sellwood stepped aside, and Flynn moved up to the counter. "Is Anna here?"

"Yeah." Sam grinned. "You're Callie's brother. The one who's a doctor."

"Yes. A surgeon."

Sam straightened. "I want to be an RN."

Maybe there was more to the young man than Flynn gave him credit for. "A worthy and necessary profession. Do you know what you want to specialize in?"

Sam sighed. "I need to get accepted into the program first before I decide anything. But working at a hospital appeals to me more than a doctor's office."

Flynn understood that. "Hospitals keep you on your toes. Good luck."

"Thanks." Sam pointed to a doorway. "Anna's in the grooming area over there."

Flynn walked through the doorway.

"Who's my good boy? Is Harley my good boy?" Anna asked a dog in what looked to be a specially designed tub. She washed him. "You smell better now. Your mama's going to be much happier. But you need to stay away from the skunks, okay? You've surely learned your lesson."

The golden retriever—Flynn recognized the breed because a neighbor owned one—soaked up the attention.

"It's about time for them to make baby skunks," she continued as if the dog understood her. "Sorry to say, those lady skunks aren't interested in what you have. Their loss. I know."

Flynn found himself smiling.

"One more rinse, and we'll be done," she added.

He moved closer.

The dog's ears perked.

Anna glanced over her shoulder. Her face dropped. "Oh, it's you." She didn't stop rinsing the dog. "Callie's not here. I don't expect her to come in today."

"I'm not here to see my sister."

Anna's gaze bounced between the dog and Flynn. "I need to dry Harley, and the dryer's loud."

Flynn had no idea what was involved in dog grooming or if Anna wanted to get rid of him, but the drying unit attached to the wall looked high-powered, so maybe she was telling the truth.

"I'm leaving today," he said. "I want to say goodbye to Taryn and Raine, too. I'll do that and come back."

Anna nodded and returned her attention to the dog. "Come on, handsome. Let's get you looking dapper for your mama."

The affection in her voice for the animal stunned him. She'd never spoke to Flynn like that. Not even close. And this big dog wasn't even Anna's, yet she acted like he was the most amazing creature known to man while ignoring Flynn, who stood right there.

He didn't get it.

Forty minutes later, Flynn still didn't understand when he called her name, and Anna ignored him. Instead, she gazed adoringly into the front window where Milo played with a Chihuahua.

He would try again. "Anna."

This time, she faced him. Her eyes widened. "Oh, I didn't know you were there."

Obviously. Flynn handed her a gingerbread latte from the coffee shop and a white bag with a cookie inside from the bakery. "These are for you."

"From Raine and Taryn?"

Of course, she would think that, which told him how far he needed to go with his apology. "From me."

"Oh." Anna studied the bag and cup. "Do I need Sam to taste them for me?"

Flynn flinched. "They aren't poisoned."

"One can never be too careful these days. And you are a doctor so probably know about medicine they can't trace through toxicology tests."

"You watch or listen to crime shows."

"Maybe. Though if something happens to me, you'll be in charge of the shower." She sipped the latte and smiled. "My favorite."

"I asked Raine what you like."

Anna's nose crinkled "Is this a thank you or something before you bolt out of town until the baby shower?"

"It's…something. A peace offering."

She held the cup in front of her lips. "Huh?"

"I'm sorry for dumping the baby shower on you and not offering to pay. And for questioning your integrity by running a background check on you."

"O-kay." Anna lowered the cup. "Apology accepted."

"That was easier than I expected it to be."

"Want me to stomp my feet and pout for a few minutes?"

"Not really."

"Didn't think so." She took another sip of her drink. A dab of whipped cream got stuck on the corner of her mouth. "Have a safe flight home."

Flynn couldn't stop staring at her lips. No, the whipped

cream. He pointed to his own mouth. "You have some…"

Her tongue darted out and licked the whipped cream away.

His temperature shot up. Must be the jacket he was wearing. He unzipped it but continued to stare, mesmerized.

"Flynn?"

Anna's voice startled him. "What?"

"Is it gone?"

Flynn blinked. Tried to orient himself. He felt as if he was in a daze. And why did he keep looking at her lips? "Yes."

"Are you okay?"

No, and he had no idea why. "I want to help with the shower. We can text or call. Video chat."

"Um, sure." She sounded anything but certain. "Why the change?"

"Callie wants me involved."

"I didn't say anything to her."

"I know." That reminded him. Flynn pulled out the money he'd withdrawn from the ATM outside the bank. "Use this to buy what you need for the shower. Let me know if you need more."

She held her cup and the bag with her left hand and took the cash with her right. Her eyes bugged out. "I don't think I've ever held this much money. Not even after manning our booth at the summer fair."

"Don't spend it all in one place."

She stiffened. "I'll send you receipts."

That hadn't gone over well. "I was joking."

"Oh."

Guess more work needed to be done. "We started off on the wrong foot, but we have time to figure things out. We both want Callie and Brandt's shower to be perfect."

"Yes, we do."

Milo jumped out of the window, ran to Anna, and barked.

Anna wagged a finger at the dog. "You're supposed to stay in the window until I take you out. Go back and play with Fred."

Milo sniffed the ground.

Flynn's gaze kept returning to Anna's face. Not only her lips, but also her blue eyes. He hadn't noticed they were blue before, had he? "Well, I should go. It's a drive to the airport."

She nodded. "Thanks for the latte, cookie, and cash. For the shower."

Something wet hit his pant leg and foot.

He glanced down. Milo's leg was raised and he peed on Flynn.

"Milo!" Anna shouted. "Stop that."

Milo did. The dog pranced like a show pony toward the window and jumped back into the play area with an excited Fred.

"I'm so sorry." Anna hurried to the counter. She placed everything on top and grabbed a roll of paper towels from underneath it. "I don't know what got into him."

Flynn stared at his wet pants and shoe. Everything would go into the trash as soon as he got clean clothes and shoes out of his suitcase to wear. "It's more like what came out of him."

Anna laughed. "It's actually a compliment."

"How so?"

"Milo must like you. He was marking his territory."

"His territory?"

"You."

Flynn side-eyed the dog who was paying no attention to him. Maybe Milo was smarter than he looked. "Lucky me."

Chapter Five

THE DAY FLEW by, the same as the ones before. Anna still had an hour or two of work to do. She wiped her forehead with the back of her hand before shelving bottles of dog shampoo. It wouldn't be much longer. No one else was coming into the shop.

A good thing.

Her ponytail had slipped two inches lower. If she had grooming appointments scheduled or customers to help, she would be more concerned with her appearance. Now, she didn't care. All she wanted to do was finish the tasks she'd started earlier and stopped multiple times throughout the day.

Callie's worsening morning sickness meant everything had fallen on Anna. She didn't mind, but things were slipping. The overnight boarding was working just fine, but someone needed to be there first thing in the morning to relieve whoever was working. Reordering products was becoming a daily task. But rescheduling grooming appointments because Anna needed to do other things she normally didn't do wasn't good for business.

Most customers understood, but others would turn elsewhere if things didn't return to normal soon. Callie was looking for additional help but finding the right people—dog people—who would work well at Wags and Tails would take time.

Until then, Anna, Sam, Mary Jo, and Becca had to keep things running smoothly for Callie.

Milo barked from the front window.

"It's okay, boy. The front door is locked." Anna glanced over her shoulder to check on him. He had his paws on the glass as people walked by on the sidewalk. "But thank you for being such a brave guard dog."

Milo's tail wagged faster.

"I'll get done as soon as I can. Your feline siblings are going to think we've abandoned them."

Her apron pocket vibrated.

Her heart jolted. *Please let it be…*

She pulled out her phone from the pocket and glanced at the screen. It was a message from Callie, not Flynn. The guy hadn't texted her since he'd left Silver Falls eight days ago. Yes, she'd been counting.

Callie: I'll be in tomorrow morning.

Anna: Only if you feel up to it.

Callie: Brandt and my family have been babying me, and this time, I've let them. Lots of women work through morning sickness. And you're right about how this could affect Wags and Tails's bottom line.

Anna: Don't push too hard.

Callie: I'm doing nothing so I can do more. I plan to interview applicants next week. Morning sickness won't last *forever, but I need to plan for maternity leave.*

Anna: *Sounds good.*

Callie: *You're there now, aren't you?*

Anna: *I'll be leaving soon.*

Callie: *There's no other issues?*

Anna: *None I can't handle.*

Anna wasn't sure if she could handle Flynn Andrews, but she didn't feel right mentioning him to Callie. The guy had sounded sincere when he apologized and offered to help with the baby shower. But he hadn't replied to any of her texts.

Not a text. Texts as in plural.

The truth was, she wanted to hear back from Flynn, and not only about the shower. It was weird and made zero sense, but when he'd been there and brought her a drink, the way he'd stared at her made her heart bump. Okay, her heart had danced like it would be going viral on every social media platform.

She'd quickly realized the reason—whipped cream on her face. But for a second, maybe a nanosecond, he'd appeared interested in her, and she'd liked that feeling. More than she thought she would.

"Stop imagining things," she said aloud.

Anna should stop because nothing would happen there. All she really wanted was a reply. She reread her text to him as if that would bring a reply.

Anna: *Have you checked your schedule? We need to pick a date for the shower.*

Anna: *Still need to set the date for the baby shower.*

Please send what works for you.

Anna: *Do you have any dates for the baby shower yet?*

With each text, the gnawing in her gut returned.

Maybe Flynn was busy getting back into his routine at the hospital. Laundry was a hassle after a vacation. She'd never taken a long one like Flynn had, but her friends complained about that when they returned home. Or maybe he received so many texts hers had been buried by others. She could easily remedy that, and she had nothing to lose.

Anna typed a message and hit send.

Anna: *Just checking in. I want to send the save-the-date emails. Send me some dates, please. Thanks.*

"Delivered" popped up below the text, but no little dots appeared saying Flynn was replying.

She sighed. Okay, an instant reply would have been too much to hope for, but a part of her had hoped that would be the case.

Always the optimist.

If only…

People kidded her about being a ray of sunshine. Little did they know she'd grown up full of dark clouds. Now, they loomed in the not-so-far-off distance, but she tried to keep them away. Flynn Andrews wouldn't be the one to bring them back.

Two days later, when he still hadn't replied with any dates, she focused on remaining patient and understanding.

"Flynn must still be busy," she said to Milo, who danced around the kitchen in hopes of getting a snack, which she gave him. Cuteness paid off. Her three cats—Bristol, Snowy, and Pumpkin—and her two fosters—Inky and Midge—all got treats too, even though all looked at Milo with a disdain only cats could pull off. "What else could be going on with him?"

As her fur babies munched their treats, she returned to the Pinterest board she'd set up for baby shower ideas. Callie and Brandt had told Anna what they wanted—and didn't want—so she'd been planning with hopes of setting the date and moving forward by now. Without a date, she could at least speak to Pippa about decorations for the party.

The next day on her lunch break, Anna entered the flower shop and inhaled the fragrant scent.

Pippa stepped out of the back wearing a vinyl apron over her floral print dress. "Hey."

"I love walking in here." Anna sniffed the air. "No wonder you became a florist."

"One of the perks. What can I do for you?"

"I need flowers and decorations for Callie and Brandt's baby shower."

Beaming, Pippa pulled out a sketch pad from beneath the counter. "I saw your Pinterest board. I've been jotting down ideas."

Anna knew she could count on Pippa. "Oh, let me see."

As Pippa flipped through the rainbow-colored decorations, Anna's heart swelled. "Everything is perfect."

"You provided the inspiration. All I need is the date."

Anna slumped. "I hope to have that soon."

"Is there a problem?"

"Not a problem, per se. I'm waiting to hear what day works best for Callie's family."

"You must mean Flynn." Pippa didn't sound impressed. "I can't imagine Raine or Taryn not being on top of this."

"It's Flynn, but I don't want Callie to know he's the holdup. I'd feel like a tattletale."

"Well, I hope he doesn't leave you to do this on your own."

Anna shrugged. "He gave me money for the shower, so there's that."

"The flowers and decorations are on me. My gift to Callie and Brandt."

"That's so nice of you."

Pippa shrugged. "Everyone's been so nice to me since I moved to Silver Falls, especially you, Callie, Raine, and Taryn. This is the least I can do."

"Thank you. Now I can splurge on the food and drink."

Pippa laughed. "Priorities. But don't forget the games."

"Oh, I haven't. The Andrews are big into games."

"I hear they're cutthroat."

"No blood or tears allowed at the baby shower."

"Better warn them about that," Pippa joked. "The brothers made bets at Raine and Keaton's wedding. Competing seems to be their thing."

"I'm surprised Flynn had time for betting. You danced with him a lot."

"We did. He's a good dancer, but that's all we did."

Anna shouldn't ask, but curiosity got the better of her. "You looked like you were having fun."

Pippa nodded. "I thought there might be more there, but when we went out to dinner the next night, he made it clear he wasn't interested in anything other than a holiday romance."

"Ouch."

"I know, right?" Pippa laughed. "There went my mom's dream of me marrying a doctor. But probably for the best."

"Why do you say that?"

"Between us, I think the only reason Flynn danced with me and asked me out to dinner was to keep Margot off his back."

"She loves to play matchmaker."

Pippa nodded. "He's not ready for that. Halfway through the first song, I knew his job meant everything to him. Flynn Andrews lives and breathes work. He even took a call in the middle of our dinner from a colleague who wanted to consult with him."

"That's dedication."

"Probably why he only wants to go out casually. He has no time or interest in anything serious."

"At least you know where you stand."

"Yep. He was open about it. So was I. No hard feelings. But it seems as if the stars and the planets must align for a romance to work."

"I feel the same way," Anna admitted. "Until I look at Callie, Taryn, and Raine. Somehow it happened for them."

Pippa nodded. "Gives me hope I'll find that too."

"Same." Anna sighed. "Is it too much to ask that more handsome, single men come to Silver Falls and decide to stay?"

"Not at all."

Anna never planned to leave the small town she now called home. She'd grown up in Southern California and was never going back. Sure, she could be one of many there. But why tempt fate? If her dad ever wanted to find her—and that was a big if—he would expect her to be there, not in a small town in Washington.

"Let me know when you have a date," Pippa said. "I have a few weddings booked, but I can work around them."

"I'll text you a list of the possible dates. Tell me what works best for you."

Pippa smiled. "I appreciate that."

As Anna walked out of the flower shop, she checked that off the to-do list on her phone.

Her satisfaction over the shower planning quickly disappeared as her phone remained silent. Two more days passed without a reply from Flynn, but she had a list of dates from Pippa, which helped Anna narrow down when to hold the shower.

As Anna sat with a plate of spaghetti and garlic bread in her kitchen, her fur menagerie waited at her feet for any crumbs to fall. Like it or not, the time had come. She stared at the message she'd typed earlier but hadn't sent.

Anna: *Haven't heard from you, and the clock's ticking. If I don't hear from you by tomorrow, I'm setting a date and hoping it works for you.*

She read the text to make sure she'd sounded nice. Not

that they'd interacted at all since he'd left, but he was Callie's brother. Once again, Anna was relieved he lived in L.A. and not Silver Falls.

She hit send and returned to her dinner. "That should get him to reply."

The cats ignored her, but Milo tilted his head as if she was living in a dream world. Maybe she was.

After dinner, Callie washed the dishes. She had a dishwasher, but since it was only her and the animals, she usually washed things by hand. As she set out the plate to dry, she glanced at her phone.

No notifications.

She didn't get many texts. A few from friends or a client with a question about their dog's coat or grooming. Tonight, her phone remained eerily silent.

"Everyone else has a life," she said to Milo.

He barked.

"Oh, I have one too—and all of you." But the dog and cats didn't reply. And Flynn…

"I thought he was being sincere with his apology. I want to give him the benefit of the doubt, but how hard is it to reply to a text to say he's no longer interested in helping?"

Milo barked again.

"I know. It's fine." It had to be. "I have a backup plan. I only hope I don't have to use it."

But after another week went by, Anna's optimism had packed up and left town, which was why she sat in Lawson's Bakery, picking at a scone, waiting for Garrett and Keaton. The two brothers arrived at the same time, went to her table, and sat.

Anna straightened. "Thanks for coming."

Garrett's brows drew together. "You said it was important."

She nodded. "Important to Callie and Brandt. It's their baby shower. Promise you won't tell her, but I can't get ahold of Flynn."

Keaton rubbed his face. "We won't say a word to Callie. But none of us can reach Flynn. He's missed our family chats. Mom said he's working crazy hours again. Still, I thought Flynn wanted to help with the shower."

"Me, too," Anna admitted. "But I don't think I can wait much longer."

"Don't wait," Garrett said, to her surprise. "Who knows when things will settle down for Flynn."

Keaton nodded. "I doubt he'll stop working like this unless Mom or the hospital force the issue. But that has nothing to do with the baby shower. Other than you shouldn't have to do everything on your own. How can I help?"

"I'm in, too." Garrett smiled at her. "Tell us what you need."

Relief pulsed through her. These two men were her plan B and it was working out better than she expected. She hadn't needed to ask for help. They'd offered.

"I need to set a date so I can mail the save-the-date notices. Flynn never gave me any times that worked for him. He hasn't replied to any text since he left."

Keaton shook his head.

Garrett's lips thinned.

"Forget about Flynn." Garrett pulled out his phone and tapped on the screen. "What date works for you, Anna?"

"Callie and Brandt gave me a list—"

"You're the one organizing this," Keaton interrupted. "So pick what works best for you."

Anna's eyelids heated. She wished Flynn was more like his brothers. "The third or fourth Saturday in April would give us time, and both dates work for Pippa. I was thinking of holding the shower at my place in the afternoon with appetizers, drinks, and desserts. No meal to keep things simpler."

Garrett studied his calendar. "I'd say the third Saturday."

Keaton had his phone out. "Works for me."

Garrett tapped on his phone screen. "I'll let our eldest brother know so he can book a flight."

Anna stared in disbelief. "Just like that?"

"Isn't that what you wanted?" Keaton asked.

"Yes, but I didn't think it would be this easy," she admitted.

Garrett laughed. "That's because you're dealing with the arrogant surgeon. Now you have the not-so-egotistical lawyer…"

"And the still-brainy professor at your service," Keaton finished for him.

Both brothers gave slight bows. She grinned at the way they'd embraced Callie's nicknames for them. Though she had a feeling Taryn and Raine had something to do with that.

A weight lifted from Anna's shoulders. "Well, thank you because I was sweating asking you guys."

"Happy to help," Keaton said.

"Anything for Callie," Garrett added. "Taryn and I will take care of the desserts."

"Raine and I can handle the beverages," Keaton offered.

"I want to order appetizers from Beth at the Falls Café so that takes care of the food. And I can figure out the games."

"Games?" the two men asked in unison.

"Games," she repeated. "Let me guess, neither of you have attended a baby shower before."

Both shook their heads.

"There will be games and prizes." Anna remembered what Callie had told her about her family's competitiveness. "But please, don't go all cutthroat on each other to win. If Callie cries, I want them to be happy tears, or Brandt won't be happy."

Garrett held up his hands. "Neither will our parents. We won't play any of the games."

Keaton's face fell. "What if we play but not like we usually do?"

Garrett shook his head. "Not possible, bro."

Keaton glared. "Yes, it is."

Garrett scoffed. "You made Callie go bankrupt twice playing Monopoly over Christmas. After the first time, you said you'd go easier on her. Then when she cried after the second time, Brandt was in your face."

"We always play hard." Keaton made it sound like a reasonable excuse.

Anna needed to shut this down. She recalled the games she'd found on Pinterest and ones from baby showers she'd attended. "What if the games are played in teams? Or people earn diaper pins and whoever has the most when we finish wins a prize?"

Keaton started to speak, but Garrett cut him off. "Whatever you think best. And we're happy to help cover any costs."

Keaton nodded. "You put on Callie's bridal shower and bachelorette party last summer."

"Thanks, but Flynn gave me money before he left," Anna said. "I'll have plenty with what you guys are providing."

"Well, this shouldn't fall only on you," Garrett said. "Just let us know if you need anything else."

"I will." Anna didn't think she would need to though. "But I appreciate you two. I was getting worried."

"You have nothing to worry about." Keaton smiled at her. "Flynn's job takes a lot out of him."

"I imagine being a surgeon would." Anna hadn't gone to college, but she understood the demands of a high-pressure job like Flynn's. Even though Dr. Rosen didn't work at a hospital, there were days he came into the shop looking exhausted from working at a small-town practice and running a weekend urgent care clinic.

Garrett nodded. "He takes on way too much, always has, even as a kid. So don't take him not responding personally."

Anna still did, but... "All I care about is making sure Callie and Brandt enjoy their baby shower."

"With you in charge, they will." Keaton glanced at her

half-eaten scone. "If there's nothing else, I want to see what my talented sister-in-law has in the display case today."

"And we mean it." Garrett scooted back in his chair. "Let us know if you need anything else."

"Will do." Anna would text Pippa the official date and order appetizers from Beth. First, she needed to relieve Mary Jo and Sam. But the shower was coming together. Flynn or no Flynn, everything would be okay now thanks to his brothers. And Callie's morning sickness wouldn't last forever. Soon, everything would be back to normal. Anna couldn't wait for that to happen.

Chapter Six

IN THE HOSPITAL'S break room, Flynn laid his head on his arms. He would prefer a bed, but he needed to see patients and possibly perform another surgery depending on the imaging results. He yawned. A few minutes of shut-eye would give him the rest he needed.

The last procedure had worn him out. His vision had blurred at the end, so he'd asked a resident to close. Something not unusual at a teaching hospital, but the circumstances hadn't been ideal. Still, no harm done. He'd supervised, and the patient was recovering well. Now for a little rest...

"Flynn."

That sounded like Mom. Flynn blinked open his eyes to find his head on his arms. Where was he?

He straightened and glanced around.

Oh, he was in the break room. He must have fallen asleep.

Flynn rubbed his sore neck. Maybe closing his eyes for a few minutes hadn't been a good idea.

"You can't keep working these hours."

There was Mom's voice again. Except he was awake now.

He glanced over his shoulder. She wore a white jacket over her clothes and leaned against the wall.

"Mom?" he asked.

"I realize your practice has staffing issues, but people have noticed how tired you are."

He stiffened. "I've done nothing wrong."

"Not yet, but you handed off a patient today."

"Not the first time any of us have done that."

"Your hand trembled. You were exhausted."

He hadn't noticed his hand. Had someone else? "Long day."

"When was your last day off?"

Flynn thought back. "I watched the two championship football games."

Since then, he'd worked out of necessity, not choice, because a partner's mother had gone into hospice. Another had experienced placenta previa and been put on bedrest. The surgeon who'd returned from maternity leave had daycare issues so was only back part-time.

It hadn't been ideal, but the remaining partners did what they could, including him. His wanting to find balance in his life had been put on hold for now. The practice had bills and a payroll to cover, not to mention a contract with the hospital.

He yawned and rubbed his eyes.

Mom sat next to him. "That was in January."

"Yeah."

Her eyes darkened. "It's early April."

Wait. What? "No, it's not."

"It is."

How had three months disappeared? He'd been working nonstop, but still…

"I'm not saying this as your mother, but as chief of staff: you're exhausted and running on fumes," she continued. "You're in no condition to perform surgeries."

She made his tiredness sound unfixable. "I just need some sleep. I took a nap. I feel better already."

She raised a finely arched brow. "From a nap, after months of running yourself ragged."

It wasn't a question. Still, he felt the urge to defend himself. "The patient came through and is recovering."

"This time, yes. You did the right thing earlier with the resident, but what if you hadn't and something went wrong? We can't afford that to happen."

"I'm doing the best I can." He couldn't hold back a yawn.

"You're trying, but that's not good enough."

Her tone sent a shiver along his spine. "What are you saying?"

"You're being put on a leave of absence. Effective immediately." She held up her hand as if to silence him. "I spoke to your partners and explained the situation. They agree."

"There's no one to pick up the slack."

"Because you were doing it. Trust me, others will step up the way they should've been doing before." Mom touched his shoulder. "If they choose not to, that's not your problem. You need to focus on you."

"I'm fine."

"You're not. Have you been taking Adderall?"

"No." His jaw tightened. "A few medical students used that, but I've never…"

"Then you'll have no problem agreeing to a blood test."

"I can't believe my own mom is accusing me of—"

"Dr. Andrews." She used her hospital administrator voice. "Trust me, you don't want to deal with my mom side right now. I must protect the hospital from any hint of wrongdoing or malpractice suits."

"By throwing me under the bus?"

"By making sure you don't get into trouble. You returned in January raring to go. People noticed the change from then until now, which is why they've spoken up. The fact you've lost track of time…"

"I get it." Flynn wasn't stupid. He'd pushed too hard if people were talking about it. Someone must have mentioned drugs, which he'd never done. Too many medical careers had gone sideward or ended from addiction. "So, what am I supposed to do?"

"Go to Silver Falls. Rest up. Help Anna with Callie and Brandt's shower. It's next weekend, in case you forgot, and your brothers said you've done nothing to help other than give Anna money before you left. Callie thinks you've been involved this entire time. Wait until after the shower to come clean. I want everything to go perfectly for her and Brandt."

Flynn rubbed his forehead. He'd meant to reply to Anna's texts. Who was he kidding? He'd meant to do a lot of things. "I didn't know Anna set a date."

"It's been mentioned on our family chat several times."

Mom's voice sharpened. "I suggest you book a ticket A-S-A-P. Margot has your room ready unless you want to stay with one of your siblings."

Flynn didn't think he could deal with the happy couples. Besides, he knew where he'd be comfortable. "Margot's place works."

"You need to step up, Flynn." Lines appeared around Mom's mouth. "Callie is over the worst of her morning sickness, but Anna's picked up the slack this entire time. Between running the doggy daycare and organizing the shower, she doesn't need any of your grief."

Mom must've heard about what happened. He swallowed.

"Yes, I know about the background check you had run on her," Mom said as if reading his mind. "Be nice to her."

"You don't have to treat me like I'm twelve."

"Then stop acting like it. With Anna and with yourself. You're no good to anyone, especially your patients, as tired as you are. Get some sleep and therapy if you think that'll help you find balance."

"I don't need therapy."

"Everyone does, but you don't get a third chance if this happens again. Too much is at stake. Given the choice between a contract with the hospital being canceled or keeping you on staff, I'll win."

Mom would never admit it, but she was more competitive than any of them. "I get it."

"You better."

His gaze met hers. He couldn't tell if she was disappointed in him or worried. Perhaps a combination of both. "I'm sorry."

"I'm sorry for not stepping in sooner." She attempted a smile, a pathetic-looking one, but a smile, nonetheless. "You need to learn balance. I'll keep saying that until it sinks in. Stop trying to be a superhero or God. You deserve to have a life outside of this hospital as much as everyone else."

Flynn didn't know what to say. A shrug wouldn't go over well, so he didn't reply.

"Go home and sleep." Mom stood. "Your dad and I will see you next weekend in Silver Falls."

"Okay, Mom." He didn't know what else to say, but he felt like a disappointment. A failure. A way he'd never felt in his life.

"This won't be easy for you, but it's for the best. We love you."

Not trusting his voice, Flynn nodded. His parents loved him, but that didn't make being put on leave any easier to accept. A part of him wanted to fight it. But Flynn had been told to find balance before. He hadn't after he'd returned in January and pushed too hard.

Yet again.

What was wrong with him? Why did he keep throwing himself into work like this? The answer came quick. He was the only single surgeon at the practice. The rest had families, but Mom was correct. He deserved a life too.

Flynn only hoped he'd get the rest he needed and figure out how to balance his life. He didn't know what he would do if he ended up in Silver Falls for more than two weeks.

"SURE YOU DON'T mind closing tonight?" Callie wiped the front counter. "You've been working so many extra hours."

Anna tidied up the front window where smaller dogs often played. The front part of the shop closed to customers, but someone on the overnight shift slept in the back so the dogs being boarded were never alone. "You've been full-time for weeks now. Enjoy a night out with your husband without having to worry if a food smell will make you nauseous."

"I never want to be like that again."

"I've heard pregnancy and labor amnesia happens to ensure the continuation of our species."

"I wouldn't be surprised if that's true." Callie rubbed her stomach. She showed more every day, and it was a good look on her. "But this one will be an only child."

Anna didn't believe that for a second. "Whatever you say."

"Margot should be by soon."

Rex hadn't come in today since Brandt worked from home. That meant only Milo, Angus, and Sadie remained at Wags and Tails. "I'm sure she'll be here any minute. Go."

Callie grabbed her jacket and purse. "See you tomorrow."

"Have fun." As Callie opened the door, the bell on the door jingled. Anna finished cleaning. She glanced at the clock.

Margot must be running late.

No worries. Anna would get the dogs ready to go home. It wasn't as if she had any plans tonight other than to eat dinner and binge a show.

As she went into the back, the bell jingled.

"That must be your mom," she said to Angus and Sadie. The dogs pranced as if excited. "I'm sure you'll get a wonderful dinner."

Milo barked.

She laughed. "You will, too."

Anna led the three dogs into the lobby. Only Margot wasn't waiting for her.

Flynn was. "Hey." His tone was casual despite having vanished more than three months ago.

The season had changed from winter to spring, but that wasn't the only difference since he'd been there the last time. Flynn appeared to be beyond tired. His complexion was pale. The lines under his eyes dark. Truth was, he looked like he'd been hit by a semitruck. Anna fought the urge to tell him to sit and to make him a pot of chicken noodle soup. But whatever was wrong with Flynn was none of Anna's business. Margot would take care of him.

"I'm here for Angus and Sadie," he said.

Anna had hoped he'd start off with an apology, but she supposed anything he said would be meaningless. "I didn't know you were coming to town early for the shower."

"Uh, yeah." He brushed his hand through his hair. "I got in yesterday."

Knowing today wasn't his first day in town shouldn't bother her, but it kinda did. She handed him the two leashes. Okay, shoved the leads into his hand.

So what? He deserved it.

"I'm ready to work on the shower," he added.

She laughed. That was the only thing to do in a situation like this.

His brows furrowed. "What's so funny?"

"You." She raised her chin. "Thinking there's still work to be done."

"The shower isn't until next weekend."

"Your family stepped up to help. So did others." Hurt flashed in his eyes, but Anna didn't care. He'd put himself in this position, no one else. "I texted you a bunch of times in January. You didn't respond, so I moved on."

A vein pulsed at his jaw. "With everything?"

She nodded. "Taryn and Garrett are providing the desserts. Raine and Keaton are taking care of the drinks. Pippa is doing the flowers and decorations. I ordered food from the Falls Café. Beth will deliver it on the day of the event."

"Where are you having the shower?"

"My place. It's not huge, but there's a deck and a nice yard for your dad and Mr. Winslow who are allergic to dogs. I plan to clean the house from top to bottom and vacuum everything, including the furniture. The buffet table and the drinks can be inside. I also have an air purifier, so the dander shouldn't bother them too much."

"I'd like to do something. Please," he added as if it was an afterthought.

"You can come over on Saturday and help decorate." Anna thought for a moment. "I could also use help picking up after everyone leaves."

"I'll do both."

"Sure."

"I mean it."

Angus barked. That made Milo bark. If Sadie could roll her eyes, she would. Anna knew exactly how she felt—boys!

"I lost track of time," Flynn added.

"It's been over three months."

"I was busy." He almost seemed to cringe. "I dropped the ball."

"That's on you, not me."

"It's one hundred percent on me. I didn't realize the shower was coming up."

"Garrett texted you. I sent you a save-the-date email."

"I didn't see, either."

"Of course you didn't."

"I'm sorry, okay?"

"No, it's not okay." Anna didn't want to listen to his excuses. "I get that you have a high-pressure job. You literally save lives. But that doesn't give you a free pass to blow off your sister's baby shower. You can apologize all you want, but your words mean nothing to me. I ran this place while Callie had morning sickness. I had my own house and animals to care for, too. Yet I planned the shower. I didn't ignore texts or forget to reply or ignore everything else in my life because I was busy."

His mouth hung open.

Maybe no one had ever spoken the truth to him. Who knew? But the guy seemed way too entitled. But again, not her problem. Yes, they would be godparents together, but enough people would be around so she would never have to interact with Flynn Andrews one-on-one. For that, she was grateful.

"I should have closed ten minutes ago, but I was waiting for Margot to pick up Sadie and Angus." Anna pulled out her phone, typed on the screen, and hit send. Flynn's phone beeped. "That's my address for the shower. Now go. The dogs must be getting hungry. I am."

Any patience she'd possessed disappeared the moment she saw him. As she stepped away from Flynn, Milo ran in front of her, and she stumbled.

Flynn reached out and caught her. "Be careful. You might hurt yourself."

"Thanks, but Milo gets underfoot sometimes."

"He's going to get the better of you one of these days."

"Maybe, but not today. Thanks for catching me." Flynn's hands were still around Anna. He was strong and warm, and it didn't suck. But it was still Flynn holding on to her. "You can let go of me."

He jerked his arms away as if he'd realized he was holding on to a stick of dynamite.

The spot where he'd touched her burned, even though fabric had separated his skin from hers. That was weird. Most likely because she hadn't been on any dates for far too long. That was all it could be.

The best thing would be to say good night. "See you before the shower."

"I'll make it up to you."

"Don't." Anna wanted nothing to do with him. "Make it up to Callie and Brandt. She doesn't know you haven't been involved."

"My mom mentioned that. I won't take credit for anything I haven't done."

"Good, because I don't think anyone would let you."

"Does that include you?" His charming grin only irritated her.

"Especially me." Anna opened the front door. "Good night, Flynn."

He slowly led the dogs toward the exit. "I know you don't believe me, but I am sorry. Those aren't only words, and I'll prove that to you. I'm not the kind of person who promises something and doesn't follow through."

"You've done it twice now, so excuse me if I don't fall for whatever you're trying to pass off as your irresistible bedside manner. Ain't going to work."

"Isn't," he corrected. "Isn't going to work."

Her muscles tightened. "Go."

He held up his free hand. "Going."

"Good." Except he took forever to walk out the door with Angus and Sadie. Any slower, and it would have been time to set up for the shower.

At least she wouldn't have to deal with him until Saturday. But for whatever reason, she glanced out the window.

"Imminent starvation." She held on to Milo's leash. "That's the only explanation for watching him leave."

Chapter Seven

THIS WAS A bad idea. Possibly the worst idea Flynn had ever had next to thinking working so much wasn't affecting him. He could turn around and no one would know he'd been there. Except Anna was hungry, and the pizza smelled delicious. Besides, what was the worst thing that could happen?

Other than Milo lifting his leg on Flynn's shoe and pants again or Anna refusing to open the door.

Flynn shifted the box to his left hand so he could knock on Anna's front door with his right. One rap of his knuckles and barking exploded. Far off, but the volume quickly increased.

Milo must be playing guard dog. The frequency of barks was impressive for a small dog.

The door opened slightly, and Anna peeked through. "Flynn?"

"You should ask who's there *before* opening the door." He'd told Callie that a hundred times. "It's safer."

"Silver Falls is the definition of safe, but that doesn't explain why you're standing on my front porch."

Oh, right. He held out the pizza box. "I brought another

peace offering."

She inhaled and practically sighed. Okay, this hadn't been a bad idea after all.

"More like an olive branch," he added. "Well, olives and pepperoni."

Her mouth dropped open. "That's my favorite kind of pizza."

"I know."

She eyed him warily.

Flynn probably should have left that part out. He rocked back on his heels. "I asked what you usually ordered."

"A surgeon who stalks. That's a new one."

He must've been working too much because his dating know-how seemed to have disappeared. Not that this was a date, but he didn't want the door slammed on his face or the pizza. "You mentioned being hungry. I figured you would feed Milo and whatever other animals you have first. Have you started cooking dinner yet?"

"No."

She pursed her lips, and he immediately remembered the dollop of whip cream she'd licked off. What would gooey cheese look like on her mouth?

"But you didn't have to bring dinner," she added.

"Want me to go?"

"No."

The word shot from her mouth, which he took to be a good sign. She used her foot and leg to keep Milo inside.

"Thank you for bringing me dinner," she said finally.

"There's enough for two." Flynn tried to sound nonchalant. He was hungry, too, but it was more than that. He hadn't liked how Anna had dismissed him so easily. Sure, he'd deserved it. But he'd expected a little compassion under the circumstances. He'd worked himself into a leave of absence while Anna's extra hours had earned her praise from his family. Talk about a double standard. "If you want company."

She glanced at the pizza box and Milo and then at Flynn. "That's a big box, and my jeans wouldn't like me if I ate all the pizza myself."

Not the invitation he wanted, but it was better than being sent to Margot's house.

Anna scooped Milo into her arms, kicked open the door wider, and motioned Flynn to come in. He hurried inside in case she changed her mind. Flashes of gray, black, white, and orange ran by. Not dogs, so he assumed she had cats, too.

She closed the door and placed Milo on the ground. The dog sniffed Flynn's shoes. Thankfully, they weren't his best or his favorite pair. He wanted to claim it was a lesson learned, but he'd put the shoes on to walk to the doggy daycare.

"Follow me into the kitchen," she said.

He did. "Nice place."

She lived in a duplex with an open floor plan. The kitchen connected to the living room, which had a gas fireplace in the corner. Everything appeared updated. The slipcovered furniture was overstuffed and covered with lots of throw pillows. A multi-level cat tree sat near a window. Balls and mice figures littered the hardwood floor.

"This is a great space for the shower." The vibe was warm and welcoming. Not so feminine guys wouldn't feel comfortable, but the décor had a woman's touch. It reminded him how he still had framed pictures leaning against the walls because he'd never taken the time to hang them. Artwork and photographs of pets graced Anna's walls and fireplace mantel. Two pictures were from Callie's wedding day, but he saw none of Anna and her family.

"You can put the pizza on the table." Anna opened a kitchen cabinet and removed two plates. "Grab what you want to drink from the fridge. I have a water for myself already."

He did. The shelves were stocked with veggies and canned beverages. Two bottles of beer sat in the back. One of those would be good, but he was too tired and driving, so chose a flavored water. "Are you sure you don't want anything else to drink?"

"Water's fine."

Flynn carried his bottle to the table, sat, and opened his drink. The lemon-lime flavor hit the spot.

She raised the box's lid and removed a slice. "I can't remember the last time I didn't have to make myself dinner."

That surprised Flynn. He assumed a pretty woman like Anna went out a lot. Unless she preferred to stay home with her animals.

He grabbed a slice. "Do you usually eat at home when you have a date?"

She nearly choked on her pizza.

Flynn jumped to his feet. Flashes of fur darted from under the table. When had they showed up? Milo remained at Flynn's feet like a sentry or a canine vacuum cleaner.

As Anna motioned him to sit, she sipped her water and then wiped her mouth. "I'm okay. Your question caught me off guard."

"Why is that?" He took a bite. The melted cheese was thick and yummy. The pepperoni had a slight peppery taste. And the olives provided the right balance.

"I haven't been on a date in a long time."

Mom and Margot had both mentioned how much Anna had been working. "Too busy?"

"At times, but the main reason is there's a limited dating pool in a town the size of Silver Falls."

"Slim pickings?"

"The slimmest," she joked. "I've either gone out with all the single men who live here, or they've dated my friends."

He knew little about small-town life other than what he'd picked up during his visits since the Christmas before last. "Did you grow up in Silver Falls with Brandt and Taryn?"

Anna lifted her pizza slice. "No."

Flynn waited for her to finish eating. "Where are you from?"

"Southern California. I much prefer the Pacific Northwest. No offense."

"None taken. Callie and my brothers would agree with you. Where in Southern California?"

"The Valley. Reseda."

"Go back there often?"

"Nope." She took another slice of pizza. "No one I know lives there any longer."

Flynn expected her to ask where he lived, but she didn't. No problem. He could keep the conversation going. "The pizza is good."

"Silver Falls might be small, but they have excellent restaurants."

The dog rubbed against Flynn's foot. "Is Milo allowed to have human food?"

"No. He has a sensitive tummy." She snapped her fingers, and Milo went to her. "But he's ever hopeful food will drop, and he'll get a snack. Usually the cats are under the table, but they hide whenever people come over. I'll lock them in my bedroom for the shower."

"You have it all planned out."

"Not my first rodeo after Callie's bridal shower and bachelorette party."

"I forgot you were in charge of those."

"They were very low-key compared to some." She reached for her water. "Callie and Brandt's gift registry info was on the save-the-date email and the invite."

"I've bought them a gift." If Flynn hadn't, his family would never let him forget it. Thanks to the gift registry, a couple of clicks on his phone, and it was done. "But I appreciate the reminder. I lost track of more than three months working too hard."

He raised his water and sipped.

"That must have freaked out your mom."

Flynn nearly spewed liquid all over the table. He swallowed and wiped his mouth with a napkin. "You could say that."

"What do you mean?"

"She placed me on leave. I can't return to the hospital until I'm rested."

"Isn't that what happened before?"

"Yes, but I wasn't officially on a leave of absence in December." The words tasted like sand. He took another sip. "If it happens again, I'm finished at that hospital."

Margot knew all the details. If Anna didn't, she would soon.

Anna leaned forward. "What are you going to do?"

"Make sure it doesn't happen again." It sounded so simple when Flynn said it like that. "I have workaholic tendencies. My work comes first."

"Must go hand in hand being a surgeon."

"Yes, but others are better at saying no to being on call or taking on extra shifts." Flynn debated whether he wanted another piece of pizza or not. His eating habits hadn't been the healthiest with his working so much. But one more wouldn't hurt him. He took a slice. "I need to regulate my time better. Find that balance everyone talks about."

Something he hadn't been doing at all.

"There are productivity or to-do apps. You could schedule your work hours and off times, so you make sure you don't find yourself with lopsided hours—or you could find another job."

"I love what I do."

"Same, but balance is a good word to have in your vocabulary."

"So I hear," he joked. "I'm working on it. I'm sure I'll manage it. You did."

"I wouldn't go that far. I worked as much as Callie needed," Anna admitted. "But it was also for a limited time frame. I told her I couldn't keep up the pace. She hired two additional employees so things won't be as crazy when she's on maternity leave."

"Smart."

Anna raised her pizza slice. "Callie is smart. I'm glad you recognize it."

"I do, but I meant you."

Her eyes widened. "Oh, thanks."

"My brothers and I are a bit overprotective."

"A bit?" Anna scoffed. "I never thought helicopter brothers were a thing until you three."

He shifted in his chair. "We're doing better."

"She told me. I must admit it's nice to see such a close, caring family."

"Have any siblings?"

"Only child." She half-laughed. "Though in full transparency, after hearing Callie complain about you, Keaton, and Garrett, I counted my blessings about not having older brothers."

"I was an only child for a couple of years, but I don't remember it. Though there are more baby photos of me than the other three."

She laughed. "I'm sure you hold those extra photos over your three siblings."

Interesting. He studied her. "Callie told you a lot about our family."

"I guessed about the pictures. She said her brothers are competitive."

"We are."

"I'll give you a heads-up on the shower games, then."

He scooted closer to the table. "What kind of games? Are there prizes?"

Anna burst out laughing. "You and your brothers are the same. Which is why some games will be played in teams. All guests will get diaper pins if they win whether on their own or with a team. At the end of the shower the people with the most diaper pins win prizes."

Prizes, huh? The shower might be more fun than Flynn thought. "So are we talking board games or card games?"

"Baby shower games."

"What are those?"

"Dirty diaper, baby food tasting, don't say the word *baby*, diaper relay, feed the baby. I have about twenty to choose from, depending on what the guests seem into."

"I don't know whether to be impressed or terrified."

"Oh, you should be very afraid of the ones I haven't mentioned," she teased. "I was when I read about them. But it's a rite of passage. And this is what Callie wants."

"That's all that matters." He wiped his mouth with a napkin. "I can't eat another bite."

Anna eyed the pizza. "There's still half a pie."

"Leftovers."

"Do you want to take some to Margot's?"

"No, thanks. She's planned this week's menu for me."

"You'll be rested and healthy in no time."

"And a few pounds heavier."

"Loosen your belt a notch or two, and you'll be good to go."

"I suppose." He leaned back. Anna made everything seem so easy. He'd thought her smiles and sunshine attitude was an act. Maybe she really was that cheerful and pleasant. "This has been nice."

She nodded and then seemed to catch herself. "Thanks for dinner. I don't get takeout unless we're having a girls' night, but it's nice not having to cook and clean up."

The urge to ask Anna out for another dinner was strong, but Flynn reconsidered. They had to get through the shower. He didn't want to do anything to cause more problems. After the party, he might consider it.

"Do you want dessert?" Anna asked. "I don't have anything from Lawson's, but there are cookies or ice cream."

He wouldn't mind spending more time with Anna, but...

"No, thanks. I should get going so I can let the dogs out. Margot had dinner plans tonight, so I'm happy I had company instead of eating alone."

"Well, sleep in if you can."

"I plan on it. Do you have to open in the morning?"

"Yes. Sam has a class. Callie gets tired if she doesn't sleep in, so Sam and I take turns opening."

"You're a good friend."

"Try to be." Anna bit her lip. "Does Callie know you're

in town?"

"Yes, but she doesn't know I was working too much."

"She'll see your exhaustion."

"I'm not planning to visit her for a few days. I hope by then I look more rested."

"She'd want to know."

"I don't want her to worry."

Anna studied him. "Then, get a lot of sleep. More than you think you need. I won't say anything unless Callie asks me, but if she does…"

"I get it." He hoped it didn't come to that. "I'll try not to live up to her nickname for me."

Anna laughed. "Good luck."

Was she making fun of him? "You sound like I need luck."

Anna winked. "You might, arrogant surgeon."

That made him laugh. "I should go."

She stood, and so did he.

Except Flynn didn't want to leave. Being around Anna made him relax. Something he hadn't expected. He didn't feel stressed, which was a new sensation.

She walked him to the door. Milo didn't follow them. He must be asleep. "See you on Saturday."

Flynn looked forward to seeing her. Way more than he should. The strange thing was the feeling had nothing to do with the shower games or the prizes or even his sister, but everything to do with the dog groomer standing next to him. He must be more tired than he realized.

Chapter Eight

ON SATURDAY AFTERNOON, the baby shower was in full swing. People stood on the deck. Others sat in chairs on the backyard grass. A few people grazed at the buffet table. The party was going better than Anna had expected. The knot in her gut lessened slightly. She went into the kitchen with three empty drink pitchers.

Anna appreciated how many of Callie and Brandt's friends and family had shown up. Thank goodness Mother Nature cooperated or her duplex would have been crowded inside. But the sun was shining; the clouds were puffy white; and the temperature in the low seventies was perfect for a spring baby shower.

Margot sashayed up to Anna. Brandt's aunt wore an aqua, light pink, and yellow ensemble with a fringed long vest that coordinated with the decorations. "If you keep throwing soirees like this shower, you're going to replace me as Silver Falls's hostess with the mostest."

Anna stood taller. She rinsed a pitcher and refilled it with iced tea. "Thank you, but you're irreplaceable."

Margot winked. "Well, you're nipping at my heels."

"That means a lot coming from you."

"Where's your cohost? Still missing?"

"Shhhh." Anna peered around Margot to make sure Callie wasn't nearby. Anna would whisper so no one else heard. "Callie isn't supposed to know what happened with Flynn."

"It's hard to keep secrets in Silver Falls."

"Well, I want to keep this one." Anna rinsed out the pitcher that had held the blue punch. She glanced over her shoulder. "In Flynn's defense, he paid for the appetizers, games, and prizes. He helped set up and even vacuumed the furniture."

Margot's gaze narrowed. "For someone who claims to dislike the man, you're quite his champion."

"Not his champion." Anna didn't want Margot to get any matchmaking ideas. "Just wanting to set the record straight."

"Now that I know you won't go after him with your dog grooming shears, I feel better telling you that Flynn could really use a friend."

Anna set the pitcher on the counter and refilled it with the blue punch. "His three siblings and in-laws are here. Plus, you."

"We're family. The poor man is beyond exhausted. All he hears from us—well, all of us except Callie—is he needs to rest."

"Not rest. Sleep." Anna rinsed out the pink lemonade pitcher. "That kind of exhaustion isn't healthy."

"Oh my."

Anna glanced over her shoulder. "What?"

Margot's blue eyes twinkled. "Do you like Flynn?"

"I barely know the man." The words came out a little too quickly. She hoped the quilter Cupid didn't notice. "If it wasn't for the baby shower..."

"The two of you will be my great-niece or -nephew's godparents." Margot became more animated. "I'm sure you'll spend *lots* of time together in the future."

"Not with him in L.A."

"Oh." Margot's shoulders drooped. "I forgot about that."

Anna nodded. "And if he was going to date anyone, it..."

"Would be Pippa."

Saying it wouldn't be *her* was one thing. Hearing Margot agree was another. Anna swallowed around the lump in her throat. "Right."

"But he still could use a friend while he was here. A man as driven as Flynn must be going crazy with his job on the line."

True, but... "He's a smart guy. I mean, he's a surgeon, right? He'll figure it out."

"I suppose he will." Margot started to speak again but stopped. "I need to talk to my brother. I'll see you later."

Margot whooshed out of the kitchen. The space seemed a tad duller without her there. Must be her colorful outfit.

Anna hoped Margot would let Flynn relax and recover and not push him toward a relationship with Pippa. Not that the florist had mentioned having a change of heart about him, but the two had chatted a while when she brought over the decorations this morning. Whether she did or not, he didn't need that right now. Anna refilled the pitcher with pink lemonade. Taryn had also provided hot tea and coffee, besides the cold drinks. Not to be left out, Keaton had brought bottles of wine and an ice chest full of craft beers.

"Need help?" Flynn asked. In his tan linen pants, a fitted short-sleeved shirt, and light brown shoes, he looked more like a model than a surgeon. Not that she knew many doctors except for hers, who she didn't see regularly due to money, rather her lack of it or a good insurance plan, but Dr. Rosen was her primary care physician if she needed one. Funny how she would take one of her fur babies to the veterinarian without a second thought when she found justifying a doctor's visit difficult.

She handed Flynn two of the pitchers. "Put these on the table, please. I'll bring the other one out."

"You've got it."

Surprisingly, Flynn had been a big help today. She hadn't been sure if he would show up. But he'd arrived early and set up the tables and chairs people had loaned her for the shower. He'd hung the pennant-style banner and fairy lights too. With the colored helium balloons clinging to the ceiling and cute floral arrangements, Anna's house had never looked cuter or more spring-like.

As she carried the iced tea to the buffet table, laughter filled the air. Callie and Brandt stood arm in arm talking to her parents and his. Both sets of future grandparents had traveled to Silver Falls for the shower.

The beaming smiles on everyone's faces warmed Anna's heart. Everything from the food to the silly games to the adorable presents had been a big hit and made Callie so happy. That was what Anna had wanted for her best friend.

Anna set the pitcher next to a platter of iced cookies. They coordinated nicely with the multiple-layer cake topped with colored sprinkles and marshmallow with a *Boy or Girl* topper. Taryn and her crew at the bakery had gone all out with cupcakes, mini parfaits, and glass containers filled with candy that Garrett had contributed.

Flynn placed the two pitchers next to the iced tea. "You did a great job with the shower."

"Thanks." Anna straightened a glass jar filled with colorful striped straws. "It was a group effort. Everyone came through, unlike the group projects in high school."

"Not quite everyone." His voice wasn't as strong as usual.

"Bank of Flynn financed this, and you helped set up."

"I got off easy."

"Don't say that until after we clean up," she joked.

Flynn laughed. "I've got you covered."

He tucked a strand of hair behind her ear.

Her heart slammed against her chest. His gesture seemed intimate not friendly, especially with the way his gaze locked on hers. She didn't know what was going on, but she couldn't look away. Okay, she didn't want to.

"I enjoyed having dinner with you the other night." Flynn's voice was rich and smooth, like the icing on the cake Taryn had baked. "I'd like to do that again."

Anna's heart lodged in her throat. Each beat resonated like a bass drum. Could Flynn hear it?

"What do you say?" he asked.

"I-I'd like that." After what Margot had said, Anna assumed he wanted someone to hang out with, not go on a date. Though a part of her wished… Stop. Pippa was more his type. "Just let me know when."

"I will." His smile took Anna's breath away. She needed to park him in the friend zone and engage the parking brake, so he didn't move from there. "I'm not sure how long I'll be in Silver Falls, but it'll be for another week or two at least."

Not long, but another dinner with Flynn was better than nothing.

Keaton entered the living room from the deck. A long strand of connected colored diaper pins he'd won during earlier games hung around his neck. The Andrews brothers had only been allowed to participate in team games. A good thing since Raine told her that Keaton had researched baby showers and been practicing the various ones he'd found on the internet. He'd even learned to put on a baby diaper by using their dog, Autumn, as the baby, which told Anna how seriously the Andrews brothers took winning.

"Are there more games to play?" Keaton asked.

"No," she and Flynn said at the same time.

"You'll be able to pick your prize soon," Anna added.

"I hope Flynn didn't buy them," Keaton said. "Not sure anyone besides Callie needs a blood pressure cuff. And you bought her two. Why, bro?"

Flynn grabbed a cookie off the platter. "One for at work and one for home. Callie's health is important."

"She'll be fine." Keaton sounded one hundred percent certain. "Even Mom thought two of them was overkill."

"I hope they are." Flynn didn't miss a beat. "Don't forget, I got them a car seat as well."

Anna wasn't sure why Callie's blood pressure mattered, but Flynn's concern touched her. Anna had no idea what his sister thought. They hadn't had time to talk.

"And, Keaton…" Wicked laughter lit Flynn's eyes. "You should compare your diaper pins with Pippa's. She has more."

Keaton sucked in a breath. "No way. But I want to make sure."

He stormed outside in search of Pippa.

"Did you annoy each other like this when you were younger?" Anna asked.

Flynn nodded. "All the time. It was worse back then."

Anna shook her head. "Poor Callie."

"We were the best brothers."

"You were." Callie came up to Flynn and kissed his cheek. "You still are. Even when you're way too overprotective."

"Older brothers are supposed to watch out for you. Mom and Dad told us that after you were born."

Callie touched his arm. "You took the responsibility seriously."

He stared at Callie's round belly. "I'm excited to be an uncle and a godfather."

Callie rested her hand on her stomach. "As long as I don't go over my due date, we'll have a spring baby."

Flynn finished his cookie. "I arrived two weeks before my due date, but many first babies are late."

"Only time will tell." Callie smiled at both of them.

"Thank you for everything. The shower has been perfect."

Anna stood taller. "Anything for you."

"Anna did most of the work," Flynn said.

She appreciated that but… "I had lots of help."

Callie shrugged. "Still, you organized it, which must have been like herding cats."

Callie wasn't wrong. Anna smiled. "I managed. And the results were worth it."

"Well, thank you." Callie hugged Anna and then Flynn. "For the shower and being the baby's godparents. I wasn't sure if you two could get along, but you've surprised me in a good way."

Anna shared a glance with Flynn, who winked at her. "Trust me, it's surprised me too."

But in a good way. A very good way.

Margot had said Flynn needed a friend. Well, Anna needed one, too, especially one who wasn't one half of a couple. Even if it was only for a couple of weeks.

THE BABY SHOWER had ended thirty minutes ago, but satisfaction still flowed through Anna. She rinsed off a platter. "I can't believe how well the party turned out."

Flynn carried the empty pitchers. "If you ever get tired of dog grooming, you could go into event planning."

"No, thanks. I love grooming too much."

He set the pitchers on the counter. "You could do both."

"Or not." Following her passion provided Anna enough to afford the rent for this place and a few extras each month.

That was all she needed. "What's left to do?"

"Not much." Flynn counted off on his fingers. "Callie took the flower arrangements home."

"They were a present to her and Brandt from Pippa."

"My brothers and I stacked the chairs and folded up the outdoor tables. The buffet table is clear except for the tablecloth."

That meant only the decorations remained. "The balloons will come down on their own. But if you could grab the stepladder in the garage and take down the banner and lights that would be great."

"I put them up. I can take them down."

A few seconds later, the door opened and closed.

Anna placed the platter in the dishwasher. There were enough items to use it today. Most things didn't belong to her, so she would return them tomorrow or on Monday.

The door opened again.

Something squeaked.

Must be the ladder.

She rinsed off the last candy jar, placed it into the dishwasher, and pressed on. "I'm going to feed the animals, then I'll be there to help you."

"No rush," Flynn said.

A few minutes later, she went out into the living room. The ladder was set up, but there was no sign of Flynn.

Something outside the slider to the deck caught her attention. Flynn was out there on his phone.

A minute or so later, he came inside. "Hey, Callie called me. My parents and Brandt's leave tomorrow. They're having an impromptu family dinner they want us to attend. Is that okay?"

Anticipation buzzed through Anna. Callie had told her about their family dinners. Anna had wanted to experience one, given she didn't have a family. She glanced at her clothes.

Her outfit had been perfect for the baby shower, but she'd worn it all day. She wanted to wear something more appropriate to fit in with Callie's extended family, but what?

Anna pictured her closet. She rarely wore anything other than jeans, but she had a black dress she'd bought at a consignment shop in Summit Ridge. It wasn't fancy but could be dressed up or down with accessories or a jean jacket. She needed shoes. Her feet ached from standing all day, but she had a comfortable pair of flats that would work with the dress.

Her stomach fluttered. "Sounds like fun."

He nodded. "Yeah, Beth had a cancellation so is able to squeeze us into the back room at the Falls Café."

"Perfect."

He glanced at the banner. "You don't mind?"

"Of course not. Family first." Someday Anna would have a family of her own. Until then she wouldn't mind being a part of someone else's family dinner. "No one turns down dinner at the Falls Café. Large party reservations are hard to come by on a weekend."

"Okay, great. I'm sorry to leave you here to finish cleaning up…"

Leave you here…

Anna's heart dropped to her feet. She wasn't invited to the dinner. Of course she wasn't. Why had she thought she would be included when she hadn't ever been before?

Because he'd said *us*.

Twice.

And she wanted to be part of an *us*.

That was all she'd wanted for so, so long.

A lump burned in her throat. Anna swallowed. "You better get going."

He smiled at her. "Thanks."

Somehow, she turned the corners of her lips upward. It wasn't easy when her eyes stung.

"I'll text you about dinner," he said.

Not trusting her voice, she nodded.

Flynn hurried to the front door, which then slammed as if punctuating the fact she was all alone again.

Only this time, colorful balloons with matching curled ribbon tails hung from her ceiling, fairy lights twinkled, and a cheery "Welcome Baby Andrews" banner hung above her fireplace.

Her chest clenched. The decorations made everything worse.

This is your life.

It always had been. There hadn't been baby or bridal showers, growing up. No family brunches or dinners or even Christmas presents. Her parents had been junkies, willing to do whatever it took to get their next fix.

Don't think about that.

Shaking off the memories, Anna climbed the stepladder.

She couldn't reach the banner so stepped up to the next rung.

Tears blurred her vision, and she blinked.

Milo barked.

"I'll be down in a minute." At least she had her fur babies. They were her family and loved her. If only they could talk back and go out to dinner with her...

She wiped her eyes and grabbed the edge of the banner.

Milo barked again.

The ladder shifted.

Oh, no. She assumed Flynn had secured it. But...

As if in slow motion, Anna reached out to the wall to steady herself. But that didn't stop the movement of the ladder.

She was falling.

Milo barked.

"Out of the way."

She hoped he would listen. Every muscle tensed.

Anna closed her eyes. This was going to hurt.

Chapter Nine

FLYNN ENTERED THE Falls Café. The place was packed with not one empty table in sight. The vibe, however, was different from restaurants in L.A. But the way the din of the customers rose with every step was the same. The hostess directed him toward the back room.

As he made his way there, people waved at him. Flynn recognized their faces. One couple had been at the New Year's Eve party, but their names eluded him. That had nothing to do with his being tired. Names flitted in and out of his mind under the best of circumstances, which was why he always reviewed a patient's chart before seeing them.

The Andrews, Winslow, and Lawson families sat around a large rectangular table in the private room. Three place settings and chairs were empty. "Way to go on getting this table tonight."

Callie's forehead creased. "Where's Anna?"

Flynn stiffened. "At her house."

Callie's mouth tightened. "You invited her, right?"

"No. You said this was a family dinner."

Everyone at the table groaned.

Flynn didn't understand. "What?"

Callie frowned. "Anna is family. I told you that on New Year's Day."

He tried to remember. "I forgot."

"I don't believe this. What else do you think I'd call my best friend who's going to be the baby's godmother? She threw the baby shower. Don't pretend you were involved in any of the planning. I heard what happened." Callie's harsh tone matched her dark eyes, causing Flynn to cringe. "I hope you didn't tell her where you were going."

He gulped.

"Guilty as charged," Garrett announced.

Flynn raised his chin. "She didn't say she wanted to come."

"Anna's not the type to invite herself." Margot sounded disappointed.

"I'm sorry." The words came so automatically, Flynn doubted they sounded sincere. But he would never hurt anyone on purpose. "I didn't know. You said family. How else was I supposed to take it?"

"Pippa's not here yet." Brandt rose. "I'll ask her to stop by Anna's place and get her."

"Thanks," Callie said to her husband, who walked out with his cell phone in hand. "Fine, I should have been clearer about who was included tonight. I'm sure she's hurting."

"Anna seemed fine when I left. She was going to take down the party decorations," Flynn said.

"You left her to finish cleaning up?" Callie's voice rose an octave. "What is wrong with you, Flynn Joseph Andrews?"

"She sounds just like Mom," Keaton said.

Garrett nodded. "Identical."

Mom beamed and raised her wineglass in Callie's direction. "That's my girl. She learned well."

As Dad and Mr. Winslow exchanged looks, Mr. Lawson laughed.

Brandt returned. "Pippa's on her way to Anna's house. I say we order some appetizers and wait for them to arrive, then we can order meals."

"Saved by the florist," Margot muttered. "You might have to do something nice to thank Pippa, Flynn."

Brandt shook his head. "Put away the arrows, Aunt Cupid. No matchmaking tonight."

Margot sighed. "You guys are no fun."

A server took their order for appetizers and drinks. The conversation quickly turned to the baby shower.

Callie's smile had returned. "I can't wait to put everything away in the nursery. Rachelle offered to install the car seat for us."

Brandt leaned lower to Callie. "I can do that, sweetheart."

"She's a firefighter," Callie explained. "The fire station does this for parents."

Flynn suddenly knew who they were talking about. Jayden, who managed Lawson's Bakery, was married to Rachelle. They'd had a baby recently. Though the passage of time wasn't Flynn's friend, so he had no idea when the couple had become parents.

Brandt's phone rang. He glanced at the screen. "It's Pippa."

"They must be having trouble finding parking," Margot said. "First Avenue is getting more crowded on Saturday nights."

Brandt took the call. His face paled. "Slow down, Pippa. What happened? Was she unconscious?"

The table went silent. Brandt touched Callie's shoulder.

Flynn leaned forward as if that would allow him to hear both sides of the conversation.

"What did the paramedics say?" Brandt asked. "No, the cats should be fine, but bring Milo. Let me ask, Callie."

"What's happening?" Callie's voice cracked.

"Where does Anna keep Milo's crate?" Brandt asked, his voice tight.

Flynn pictured a gray carrier. "I saw one in the garage when I brought in the stepladder."

"Check the garage," Brandt said into his phone. "Are you okay to drive? Okay, we'll meet you at the hospital."

Callie's eyes gleamed. "What's going on?"

"When Pippa got to Anna's, Milo was barking like crazy, but Anna didn't answer the door. It was unlocked so Pippa went in. Anna must have fallen taking down decorations. She was on the floor. So was the stepladder."

Every one of Flynn's muscles tightened. He was the one who'd brought in the stepladder. Anna had asked him to take down the banner and lights. But he hadn't.

My fault.

This was his fault.

"How's Anna?" Mom asked. "You mentioned something about her being unconscious."

"Anna was out of it, but Pippa didn't know if she had totally lost consciousness. Pippa called nine-one-one."

Something kicked in with Flynn. He stood. "Most likely a closed head injury. They'll need a CT scan to rule out anything serious."

Mom rose. "What hospital?"

"The closest one is in Summit Ridge." Margot's voice sounded shaky. "I'll go with you."

"I'll take care of the bill." Mr. Winslow pulled out his wallet. "And meet you at the hospital."

"We can drive you," Mr. Lawson offered.

"Let's go," Callie implored Brandt.

"Should you call Anna's family?" Flynn asked.

"She doesn't have any," Margot said.

Callie raised her chin. "Except us."

Taryn and Raine were already out the door. Garrett and Keaton hurried to catch up with them.

"You can ride with us." Callie grabbed Flynn's hand. "Let's hurry. You and Mom need to make sure Anna gets the best care."

Flynn nodded. If it weren't for him, Anna would be at the table with them instead of riding in the back of an ambulance.

How would he ever make this up to Anna?

FLYNN HAD STARTED rotations during his third year of medical school at age twenty-five. For nearly thirteen years, most of his time had been spent in hospitals. But this was the first time he'd been stuck in the waiting room. He hated every nanosecond of it.

He glanced at the clock that moved slower and slower, as if moving through sludge. "It shouldn't take this long."

"Welcome to the real world of medicine," Dad said. "It's different when you're on the other side of the doors."

Mom nodded. "Remember how you feel. It'll help you understand your patients' families better."

Understand what? Flynn was about to lose his mind.

Mom motioned him over to where she sat next to Dad. "You blame yourself for what happened to Anna."

Flynn didn't say anything. He couldn't, but he nodded.

"Accidents happen."

"She asked me to take down the decorations. I brought in the stepladder. I didn't invite her to the dinner."

"This is why I put you on a leave of absence, honey." Mom's voice was soft and compassionate. She held his hand. "People can get hurt when a doctor isn't on top of his game. A few nights of sleep aren't enough to say you've recovered. You're still exhausted and running on fumes. That's why you failed to realize Anna is family after all she's done for Callie."

He hung his head. "I'm not supposed to mess up like this."

"It might surprise you, but you're only human. And that's what humans do. Mess up. Doctors included."

"Not you."

"Oh, honey. Do I have some stories for you." His mom half-laughed. "This isn't the time or the place. Just know mistakes happen, especially when a person's cognitive abilities aren't functioning as usual from fatigue. You're a wonderful surgeon, one of the best I've seen, who's helped many patients. You're an even more generous man. I know you're helping that teen at the bakery with his college expenses. So cut yourself some slack."

"But Anna—" The thought of her with a TBI... He rubbed his face. "Brain injuries are—"

"Until imaging and test results come back, we have no idea about Anna's condition. Be patient and don't assume the worst, okay?"

He nodded. "It's easy to think the worst."

"And now you know how every patient's family feels. Not a good feeling, is it?"

"No."

"Go sit. Try to relax."

Flynn glanced around. Many of the chairs were filled with people who'd been at the dinner. Others were strangers, waiting for news about their loved ones.

One thing was the same—the worry.

Deep lines on faces, wet eyes, and sniffling that had nothing to do with being sick. Though he didn't doubt this place was full of germs. It was the last place Callie should be right now.

He went over to her and Brandt. "Go home."

Callie's eyes were red and swollen. She shook her head. "I can't leave Anna."

"You've had a busy day with the shower." He kneeled next to her. "And out in the parking lot, a little dog's in a carrier wondering what's going on."

Yes, Flynn was playing the dog card. That was likely the only thing to get Callie to go home before she got too tired or caught a cold or something worse. She could be upset at him later.

Callie inhaled sharply. "Milo must be so scared. Anna never leaves him in the car alone. But I don't want to leave Anna alone, either. I'm her emergency contact."

Flynn touched Callie's arm. "Anna won't be alone. I'm staying."

Callie stared at him through wet, spiked eyelashes. "Promise?"

"Promise." Flynn wasn't leaving unless they threw him out. He stood. "I'll call if we hear anything."

"No matter what time?" Callie asked.

Brandt tilted his head. "Flynn can call me, sweetheart. You need your rest. If it's important, I'll wake you."

"Okay," she said, hesitantly. "I'll say good night to everyone."

Brandt mouthed *thank you* to him.

Flynn nodded. He walked to the far side of the waiting room. An elderly man with thinning gray hair and wire-rim glasses clutched a floral scarf with a gnarled hand. A wooden cane rested against his side. He had a distant, almost haunted look in his eyes.

Something about the guy bothered Flynn. "You okay, sir?"

"No, not okay." The man focused on Flynn. "But I hope to be. That depends on Daisy. She's back there. Her heart, again. Those doctors take their sweet time, not realizing how horrible waiting for news is. Guess they must be busy."

Flynn hoped so because he finally understood the agony of not knowing what was happening behind those closed doors. "It's the worst."

"Daisy is my life. She means everything to me." The man's hands shook. "The air I breathe and the sun that provides light pale in comparison to her."

"She sounds special."

"She is the definition of the word. Been with her for more than sixty years. I want another sixty, but I'll be happy with whatever time we get together."

"I hope she's okay."

"Who are you waiting for?"

"Anna. She's sweet. A dog person."

The man laughed. "Daisy's a crazy cat lady. I swear there were plenty of times I thought she'd replace me with a new feline."

"Anna has cats, too."

"Double the trouble." The man snickered. "But I bet your lady is worth it."

"She is." *Wait.* Anna wasn't Flynn's anything. Yet the words had tumbled out like spring runoff toward the huge waterfall the town was named after.

Guilt.

That would explain it.

Except he liked the sound of his lady.

"Flynn," Dad called after him.

"I have to go," Flynn said to the man.

"Take care. And remember, no matter what happens, to

hold on to each other. It's too easy to let go when things get rough. I almost did that, but Daisy held on to me. Smart woman."

"Thanks." Flynn hurried over to his family who all stood, listening to a doctor, dressed in blue scrubs. The guy had to be younger than Flynn. He might even be a resident, and that bothered Flynn more than he wanted to admit. Anna deserved the best care.

He focused on the doctor's words. Closed-head trauma confirmed with the CT scan. Forearm sprain or fracture. Another X-ray will be needed once the swelling has gone down. Immobilized with a splint. Keeping her overnight for observation. She got lucky. It could be much worse.

The final phrase looped in Flynn's brain.

A concussion was considered a TBI, but that was better than a brain bleed or swelling.

"We're moving Anna upstairs." The doctor glanced around the group. "We allow one family member to stay with patients overnight."

"Flynn should stay with Anna," Margot said.

"Flynn's related to Anna?" the doctor asked.

"Boyfriend," Margot blurted. She glanced around. "Doesn't everyone think it should be Anna's serious boy friend who stays the night?"

Flynn couldn't believe she was trying to play matchmaker even now. "Margot—"

"You're practically *family*." Margot emphasized the last word in a way that couldn't be misinterpreted. This had nothing to do with her being a Cupid wannabe and everything to do with having someone with Anna, who had no family, and whose emergency contact had left. He'd promised Callie he would stay.

Flynn stepped forward and winked at Margot and his family. "You're correct. I should be the one to stay with my...girlfriend."

Confused glances met his, except for one.

Margot's blue eyes twinkled. She gave him a slightly concealed thumbs-up sign. "Go with the fine doctor. Anna needs you. I'll take care of things out here."

Flynn followed the doctor without another word to his family. He didn't want to give them the chance to mess this up, so Anna ended up alone tonight. Some hospitals had strange rules about visitors. He had no idea about this one, but Margot seemed to know. Even though it went against his better judgment, he would trust her tonight. For Anna and Callie's sakes.

THE NURSE DIMMED the lights in room 323, which was the last place Flynn expected to be tonight. He'd lost track of how long he'd sat there, but his eyes adjusted to the darkness quickly. Something Anna wouldn't be able to do quickly with a concussion. Any brightness would cause her pain.

The pupil dilation checks had been extended from every thirty minutes to an hour with vitals taken at the same time. A cardiac monitor sat next to the bed, but it wasn't hooked up. The automatic blood pressure cuff was on Anna's right arm and it beeped when they took a reading. A pulse oximeter was on one of her fingers. And an IV on the top of her right hand. His gaze kept straying to the bandage on her head, the bruise on her face, and the splint on her left arm that ran from her elbow to her fingertips. Not one bone was able to move.

He hoped it was only a sprain and not a fracture, but he understood the care they took. Anna earned her living with her hands. The same as him, he realized with a start. They both had that in common. Flynn held out his hand. An injury that made his hands unusable would shatter his world. He hoped Anna didn't panic when she was more coherent.

He sat in a chair on the right side of Anna's bed. No matter how many times he repositioned himself, he couldn't get comfortable. The sleep chair wasn't so bad when fully reclined—he'd napped in one in the break room at his hospital on more than one occasion—but he doubted he would sleep tonight.

Careful not to disturb the IV, he carefully held her hand, gently rubbing her skin with his thumb. He wanted to see her open her eyes. She had done that a few times, but she must be tired. Her chest rose and fell, but even in the dim lighting, the bruising on the left side of her face kept getting worse.

He'd told many families to talk to patients. That they would be able to hear them even if they didn't remember. But some did.

But now, sitting there, his advice felt stupid.

What was he supposed to say to Anna?

He didn't know where to start, yet other people did this.

Flynn took a breath and then another. "Hey. It's me. Flynn."

She didn't move. Okay, he didn't want to disturb her sleep. But he wanted her to be okay. The prognosis was positive, but he wanted guarantees. He had one of the best records at the hospital. People asked for him to be their surgeon.

You're not Anna's doctor.

Even if he wanted to be, he couldn't be hers. He knew her. She was…family.

"You were invited to the Falls Café, but I didn't realize you were included." The words poured out. "If I had, none of this would've happened. I'm so sorry."

He cringed.

"I've said those words more to you than anyone in my life, but I am sorry. You don't deserve this. Not after you asked me to take down the banner and lights. But I left them for you. This is my fault. All my fault. I'll do what I can to make it up to you. I promise, Anna. You must believe me."

Anna's lips curved upward in a serene smile. She resembled a storybook princess.

Something shifted in his chest. Flynn rubbed the spot above his heart with his left hand. With his right, he ran his finger along the side of the right side—the unbruised side—of her face.

"You're beautiful. I don't think you know that, but it's true. Just ask Milo. And your cats." Flynn couldn't remember their names—if he'd known them to begin with. "They see your beauty. They see you. So do I."

Her eyelashes fluttered like butterflies' wings.

He leaned closer. "Anna?"

"Am I dead?"

He startled. "What? No. Why would you ask that?"

"Because you're talking so sweet to me." Her voice was quiet but raw. "Water?"

A cup with a straw sat on the bed tray, but he needed her to sit up. He could do that by raising the bed. "Let's elevate you a little."

He pressed the button.

"Am I dead?" she repeated.

"No, you're in the hospital."

"Not dead."

"Very much alive." He held the straw to her mouth. "Small sips. You have a concussion so you might get sick to your stomach."

"Ugh. I hate throwing up." Still, she took a sip.

He tried not to smile. "Most people do."

The straw slipped from her lips. "Where am I?"

"The hospital in Summit Ridge."

She seemed to consider that for a moment. "What happened?"

"You fell off the ladder and hit your head."

"I don't remember."

"You don't need to now."

"Will I ever?"

"I don't know, but if not, everyone will help fill in any gaps." He would, even if it made him look like a jerk. "You need to rest."

"So do you." Her lips formed a perfect O. "My fur babies."

"Milo is with Callie. The cats are alone tonight, but Sam will go over there in the morning to feed them."

Tears gleamed in her eyes.

He leaned closer. "Do you hurt?"

"Sorry," she whispered.

"Shhh. You have nothing to be sorry about."

"You can go." Her voice cracked.

"I'm staying." He touched the right side of her face as if he'd done it a million times before. "There's nowhere I'd rather be right now."

Her gaze met his. She looked so sad and vulnerable it nearly ripped his heart out of his chest.

"Promise." He kissed her right cheek. "Sleep. I'll be here when you wake up."

Chapter Ten

"WHERE AM I?"

The question startled Flynn. His eyelids sprang open. His neck and back ached, which suggested he'd fallen asleep, sitting up. He blinked, taking a moment to orient himself. Room 323. Anna's room. He stared at her in the hospital bed.

The vulnerability on her face, not much different from a few hours ago, brought a protective instinct, an intense one he'd only felt for his family. Despite what Callie said, Anna wasn't his family. Yet that didn't stop him from wanting to crawl into the bed and hold her. He hated when a patient's loved one did that, but he understood their motivation now.

Flynn leaned forward, concerned by Anna's pale face and dark bruises. He reached out to her but then pulled back his arm. Nothing he could do to make her better right now, but he could answer her question.

"Hey, good morning." He kept his tone light and quiet. Even a normal speaking voice would hurt her head. "You're at Summit Ridge Hospital. You have a concussion."

He could almost see the gears in her brain working, but not quite clicking together as they should. She'd asked the same question each time she woke through the night.

The corners of her mouth turned down. "I don't re-member."

"That's normal." Except saying those words only intensi-fied his guilt. He would make this up to Anna, somehow.

The tension on her face remained. "Nothing's normal."

She was correct. He sat taller as if that would take some of his blame away. It didn't.

Your fault.

Flynn would find a way to make this up to her. He'd been thinking about that last night. Callie might have an idea of something he could do. "It will be after you have time to recover."

She appeared to ponder his words. Then, her eyes wid-ened, and she gasped. "My fur babies."

Of course, she would think about her dog and cats. "Don't worry about them. Callie has Milo at her house. Sam checked on the cats this morning."

"Oh, okay." She looked anything but okay.

She blinked. Her expression went blank. He recognized this look and knew what was coming next.

"You're at Summit Ridge Hospital," he said before she could ask the question again.

"How did you know…"

"You've asked me a few times, which is totally normal with a concussion."

"I don't remember." She grimaced. "I already said that."

"It's fine." He didn't want her to feel bad about repeat-ing herself. She'd injured her brain and was fortunate things weren't more serious. "You were taking down decorations from the baby shower and fell off the stepladder."

He fought hard to keep his tone steady and not cringe with each word.

Two lines formed above the bridge of her nose. "It hurts to think."

"Then don't." Flynn wanted nothing more than to erase the concern from her eyes. She had to be scared. "Do you feel you got enough sleep?"

"I..." She appeared to consider the question. "I don't think so."

"The nurse came in every hour to check your vitals, so I'm assuming you didn't."

"You must be tired."

He was, but... "I'm used to it."

"You're here to rest. Go home."

Her sharp tone surprised him, but no way was he leaving her. It wasn't only his promise to Callie. He felt responsible for Anna. "Soon. Rest. Hospitals aren't a good place to sleep."

"I'm in the hospital," she murmured as if talking to herself.

Anna closed her eyes. Her sad expression about ripped his heart from his chest. His pulse kicked up.

He had no idea what had just happened, but something had.

Do something.

Except his training wouldn't really help her. His bedside manner was presenting fast. No one would call his approach endearing. Still, he had to try. The way he had last night.

Anna deserved compassion and so much more.

Flynn covered her hand with his. The gesture seemed useless. The way he felt helpless right now. It was an odd place to be, given his job was to make patients better. Save them if need be. But seeing her like this almost defeated him.

Something twisted in his gut. "Anna?"

She opened her eyes that brimmed with tears. "Hospitals are expensive."

The rawness to her words made him squeeze her hand. "Hey. Don't worry about that. Insurance will cover it."

"No. I need to go home."

"The doctor will be by soon."

"Please. I must get out of here." She became agitated, speaking as if a period followed each word. She tried to sit up, but her grimace told him the pain kept her horizontal. "I can't stay here. This will bankrupt me."

Her words hit him like a left jab. She was worried about the bill, about money. Flynn had never worried about insurance. The thought had never crossed his mind. Growing up in Beverly Hills, he was accustomed to having it all: a family, education, important career, and insurance. Whereas Anna had an hourly job, rented one half of a duplex, and must only have a catastrophic insurance plan with a high deductible or possibly no insurance at all.

And once again, he'd assumed she was just like him. At least he knew something he could do for Anna to begin making amends.

People complimented Flynn on his generosity, but what

most didn't realize was he had more money than he had time or interest to spend it. Sure, he helped Brecken with his community college expenses, but he didn't miss the money. He would do the same with Anna's hospital bill.

The accident wasn't her fault. She shouldn't suffer any consequences for Flynn's lapse. And she wouldn't.

His respect for Anna grew. She was the definition of scrappy. He still didn't know her past, but one thing was clear. She'd made a life for herself in Silver Falls, giving her time and talents when she had so little compared to many of her friends.

"Don't worry about the cost." No one would be the wiser if he paid the bill. That was the least he could do. "Just focus on getting better."

The door to the room opened. Doctor Wingate, the same doctor from last night, walked in. He wore a white coat over his khaki pants and polo shirt. He looked as if he'd just finished eighteen holes of golf on his way in. Each of Flynn's nerve endings went on alert.

How old was this doctor?

The guy looked like an idiot. His posture suggested he had a stick up his rear. "Good morning. I hope everyone slept well."

"I've slept in worse places," Flynn said in a nonchalant tone. "Anna's been in pain from her head injury. I mentioned it to the nurse. At three o'clock, she reached for her left arm with her right hand. She wiggled her left fingers. Of course, that doesn't mean she didn't fracture anything."

"A fracture?" Anna tried to raise her head. "Is that why

my arm feels so heavy?"

"You're…" he and Dr. Idiot said at the same time.

Flynn motioned for the guy to go ahead. He was the physician in charge of Anna's care, even if he looked more like a frat guy looking for his next party.

"The X-ray was inconclusive," Doctor Idiot said. "We discussed this last night, but I'm not surprised you don't remember. I splinted your arm, and you'll have another X-ray in a day or two after the swelling goes down."

Anna bit her lip.

"It'll be okay," Flynn assured her. "You'll have the best of care. I promise."

Dr. Idiot looked at him. "Your girlfriend's lucky to have someone so devoted to her well-being."

Anna's eyes widened. "Flynn?"

The doctor's innuendo bristled. He patted her hand. "That's what good boyfriends do. Especially ones who are surgeons."

Anna gasped. Her face paled. She squeezed her eyes closed. "Dizzy."

Flynn held her hand. "Are you going to be sick?"

She squeezed his hand tightly.

"Anna?" he asked.

"I-I don't know." She opened her eyes. "Bathroom?"

Dr. Idiot handed Anna a blue emesis bag. "Use this if you need to vomit. But after last night, there can't be much left in your stomach except bile."

"I don't remember any of that." Anna clung to the bag as if she were afraid to drop it. She rolled onto her right side, but she cringed the entire time.

"That's normal with a concussion," Dr. Idiot said.

Flynn fought the urge to tell the guy to shut up.

"Let me help you." He held on to the bag with Anna. Her skin was cool against his. He would ask the nurse to get her a new blanket, one that had been heated. "Give yourself a minute. Just breathe."

Anna did. Her breaths came slower.

"Better?" Flynn asked.

She sniffled. "A little."

"You might not remember me examining you last night, but I'm Doctor Wingate," he explained in a low tone. At least he knew anything louder would be like a jackhammer to her skull. "So you're dizzy this morning."

"Yes. Confused, too," she admitted.

Hearing her called his girlfriend probably hadn't helped matters.

"Let's do a quick check," Dr. Idiot said. "What's your name?"

"Anna Kent."

"Where are you?"

"A hospital in Summit Ridge," she answered.

Dr. Idiot nodded. "Do you know why you're here?"

"I fell."

"What day is it?"

An answer didn't come straight away. "Sunday?"

It was more of a question, but Flynn was relieved she had gotten the answer right.

"Follow my finger with your eyes," Dr. Wingate said.

Anna tried, but she grimaced.

Flynn pushed his way between the bed and the idiot doctor. "Stop. She's hurting."

"Anna's doing better than she was last night." Dr. Idiot smiled at her. "Your symptoms are normal, and I'll be discharging you today, but you can't stay alone. It's not only your head, but you won't be able to use your left arm or hand with that splint."

"I need both of my hands for work." Anna's words flew out. "Our clients and my boss are counting on me."

Flynn squeezed her hand. He wanted to comfort her, but he had no idea how. "Callie understands. You need time to heal."

Dr. Idiot nodded. "Listen to your boyfriend."

"Boyfriend?" she asked, obviously still confused.

Flynn raised her hand and kissed it. Her skin smelled like sunshine. When he lowered it, he didn't let go. "This is a lot for you to take in, sweetheart, but I'll do whatever I can to help."

Dr. Idiot beamed. "I'm happy to hear that because Anna needs rest. She also needs a follow-up appointment with her primary care physician. She'll need another X-ray taken of her arm. It appears to be a bad sprain, but the radiologist's report said the swelling interfered with the imaging so there could be a fracture."

"Not a problem." Flynn didn't miss a beat. "One PCP and X-ray this coming week."

"A group of women want to come in," Dr. Idiot said. "I said I had to see you first."

Anna blew out a breath. "My friends."

The doctor nodded. "They keep asking about you, but—"

"HIPAA," Flynn interrupted.

Dr. Idiot nodded. "That's not stopping them from making plans about Anna. I wanted to warn you."

"Thanks." Anna glanced at the door. "How long do I need to have someone with me?"

"Normally, forty-eight hours, but given the splint and the fact you may end up in a cast, you might need extra help. For the first seventy-two hours you should rest. You may experience more nausea, headaches, mood swings, and fatigue. I recommend taking the week off from work. Your primary care physician may want you out longer, depending on how you heal, but I'll leave that up to them. Understand?"

"Yes," Anna said.

"It can take a month to six weeks to get back to normal, but in some cases, symptoms linger," Dr. Idiot explained. "The nurse will go over everything with you and your boyfriend before you're discharged."

"T-thanks." Anna's voice was off.

"Can you give us a minute before you let in the others?" Flynn asked.

"Of course. Take care, Anna." With that Dr. Idiot left.

Good riddance. Flynn really didn't like the guy.

He waited for the door to click shut. As soon as it did, he looked at her. "You must be confused."

"And not only from the concussion. Boyfriend?"

Of course, she would remember that part. "The hospital

only lets family stay overnight. Margot told them I was your boyfriend so you wouldn't be alone."

"Oh." Anna bit her lip again. "Thank you. I'm sure you were uncomfortable."

"Not as much as you were." He smiled at her. "I'm glad I could be here with you."

She stiffened. "I'm fuzzy about what happened last night. I remembered something though. You left for a dinner."

He hung his head. "About that. I messed up. You were invited to the dinner."

Anna's lips parted into a perfect O again. "I was?"

Her surprise was like a dagger to his heart. She might not remember, but she must've been hurt. Was that why she fell?

No, that wasn't the reason. He needed to take responsibility for this.

Flynn nodded. "You're considered family, but I took the invitation literally. I did the same thing when Keaton returned to Silver Falls last November. I'm sorry if I hurt your feelings. And for leaving you alone to take down the decorations. If I hadn't…"

"Oh. I hadn't thought of that."

Of course not. Because Anna wouldn't. She wasn't a con artist or scammer like he'd thought. But he needed to tell her this because she deserved to know and maybe she would find it in her heart to forgive him.

"Callie…everyone was upset at me," he admitted. "Pippa found you on the living room floor unconscious. The stepladder had fallen over, too. It sounded like you were taking down the decorations you'd asked me to clean up."

"I remember asking that and then you leaving, but nothing else."

"You might not ever remember. It just depends."

"On what?"

"Your brain." Flynn brought her glass of water closer and placed the straw against her lips. "Take a sip."

She did.

"Let's see if the water makes you nauseous." He didn't lower the cup. "If so, I'll ask for a second opinion as to whether you should be discharged."

"I want to go home."

"You heard the doctor. You'll be going home today."

Though Flynn didn't one hundred percent support the discharge. He wanted to make sure Anna was ready.

The door opened.

Flynn put his finger against his lips. "Talk softly, please."

Margot, Callie, Taryn, Raine, and Pippa filed in. All wore the same concerned expression.

"Your mother will be in shortly," Margot said to Flynn in a low voice, just above a whisper.

Callie's lower lip quivered. "I'm so sorry, Anna."

"No one's fault," Anna said. "Accidents happen. It wasn't Flynn's fault either."

Hearing her say that brought a tsunami of relief.

Taryn nodded. "I'm grateful Pippa found you so quickly."

"We all are," Raine agreed.

"I must've lost ten years off my life seeing you on the floor like that." Pippa rubbed her arms. "Milo was barking more than usual so I knew something was up. Smart dog."

"He's at our house," Callie said as if anticipating Anna's next question. "Sam's been to your house to feed and play with the cats. Everyone's doing fine though they took a little coaxing to come out from under your bed."

"Thanks." Anna's eyelids appeared to be getting heavy. "Flynn told me everyone stepped up."

"Come sit, Callie." Flynn motioned to the chair he'd used. He didn't like the dark circles under his sister's eyes. He got it. He really did, but she needed to be careful.

Callie made a face. "I'm pregnant, not sick."

"You had an eventful day, dear," Margot said. "Humor the doctor and me."

Callie rolled her eyes, but she sat in the chair.

"Anna will be discharged this morning." Flynn hadn't left her side, but she needed her friends more than she needed him. He took a step away. "She can't be left alone."

"Your mom thought that might be the case." Margot rubbed her chin. "She's welcome to stay at my place, but I have stairs and am gone during the days."

"I want to go home." Saying the words, Anna sounded as if she were speaking underwater. She was clearly so tired. "My dog and cats…"

"Oh, right," Margot said. "You have cats. Sadie and Angus have never met any cats."

"We can take shifts," Raine suggested. "Though daytime will be harder. I can see if someone can cover for me."

Taryn nodded. "I could do that at the bakery, and we could split the time."

"I could do some evenings," Pippa offered.

Callie smiled. "Me, too."

"Thanks, but I just need someone with me today. I'll be at work on Monday," Anna said.

"No," they said at once.

Anna grabbed her head. "I don't have a choice. I can't go without a paycheck, not with rent due and paying for this stay."

"Don't worry about that." Flynn didn't want her to worry when he planned on paying the bill.

Callie nodded. "We can figure that all out later. Right now, you need to get better."

"I have an idea." Margot's blue eyes twinkled. "Flynn needs to rest, too. He's the perfect person to stay with Anna."

Flynn flinched. "What?"

"And don't forget, he's a doctor," Taryn reminded everyone.

Raine nodded. "We can relieve him when he needs a break."

Callie's lips parted. "He won't have to juggle work, either."

"No," Anna and Flynn said at the same time.

The others talked over him and Anna as if they hadn't said a word.

Taryn's smile widened. "This is a great idea. It would give him plenty of time to rest."

"I agree," Margot said.

"Anna is about as low-maintenance as they come," Raine

added.

Pippa laughed. "Except Milo is the definition of extra, though he's now a hero in my book."

Flynn rubbed his chin. His razor stubble scratched his fingertips. "I'm not a dog person."

"Nonsense." Margot waved her hand as if swatting a fly. "You're wonderful with Sadie and Angus."

"And Rex," Callie chimed in.

"And Autumn," Raine added.

"I'll be fine," Anna said, but even Flynn could tell she was only saying the words. There was nothing in her tone to back them up. "I don't need someone—"

"Doctor's orders," her friends said in unison.

Anna cringed.

"Oops. Sorry." Raine lowered her voice. "We'll be quieter."

"Thanks." Anna looked at Flynn. "You okay with this?"

Was he? Flynn didn't know, but staying with her would be another way to make amends. He only hoped that would be enough. "Yeah, I'm good with it if you are."

Chapter Eleven

FLYNN HAD PERFORMED surgeries with backup generators providing power. He'd saved a woman's life in the emergency department's parking lot. He'd worked multiple-casualty tragedies from car accidents to shootings. No matter the situation or how tired he might be, the hospital was where he felt the most comfortable. It was his territory—his home. But this…

Callie gave him a slight push. "Go on in."

Inside.

To Anna's place.

It shouldn't be a big deal. He'd been to her house twice before—only this time he was staying longer than a few hours. Flynn clutched the handle on his rolling suitcase. He'd much rather be in the OR dealing with a rush of trauma cases. That was his wheelhouse. Providing care and comfort, not so much.

He stopped a few feet from the porch. The *Welcome* sign from the baby shower still hung on the door, sending a familiar wave of guilt through him. He'd stayed with her at the hospital and paid her bill, but those things were easier than this.

Flynn let go of his suitcase, parking it in the center of the walkway, as if the obstacle would block his and Callie's path.

"I'm not the right person for this," he admitted finally.

Callie shook her head. "We all know you are."

The ubiquitous *we*. Callie and the others had planned everything. His mother had agreed. And Margot...

His staying with Anna had probably been Margot's idea.

"Margot's playing matchmaker." The words shot from his mouth like blood from a severed artery. Only this wasn't something he could fix. "Her eyes were twinkling the way they do whenever she talks about the couples she's set up or wants to."

Callie laughed. "Don't be silly. Margot's relieved Anna will be okay. It might be difficult for you to check your ego at the door, but please do. You and Anna are like chalk and cheese. Margot sees it too. She continues to have high hopes for you and Pippa deciding you want to be more than friends now that you're in town."

His jaw tightened. He'd enjoyed spending time with the florist, but they wanted different things. Not to mention, he was only staying in Silver Falls a short time. "Not going to happen."

"That's what I told her." Callie didn't sound upset. "Even though Anna's my best friend, and the two of you are getting along better, I can't see her with you and vice versa. Do you want me to say anything else to Margot?"

"No." Though he and Anna had never been that bad. They hadn't really known each other. "I assumed Margot was up to her old tricks because Keaton and Raine are opposites."

"Opposites who had a spark from the beginning, even if they wanted to pretend it wasn't there."

"Right." Except Flynn had felt a spark with Anna. Unless he'd imagined it. If so, all his worries were for nothing. Not that he was worried now. He wasn't now that Margot wasn't playing matchmaker. Yet, spending time with Anna still didn't seem like the best idea.

"And you're a doctor," Callie added. "That's the other reason you should be the one to stay with Anna."

"I'm a surgeon, not a family practice MD or an internist." As soon as the words left this mouth, Flynn realized he must sound snobby. "Anna would be better off with someone…softer."

So long as it wasn't Doctor Idiot. Wingate kept eyeing Anna as if he wanted to take her home. So unprofessional. Or that paramedic who'd stopped by to check on her while they'd waited for her to be discharged. That guy was way too smooth and after only one thing. Anna didn't need Flynn; she needed a bodyguard.

Callie rolled her eyes. "You may be arrogant or grumpy at times, but you're more qualified than any of us."

Her gaze narrowed. She studied him as if he were a critical patient's blood test report. "What's really going on?"

The collar around his neck tightened. Or it would have if he wasn't wearing a V-neck T-shirt. Seeing Anna in the hospital bed had shaken him to his core. He'd had to remind himself to breathe and not demand to see her chart then and there. He'd gotten so frustrated when Anna was in pain and the third shift nurse didn't answer the call button fast enough. He'd wanted to hold Anna until the confusion in her dilated pupils vanished.

The dog groomer who was all sunshine and rainbows made him feel things he wasn't used to feeling. He wasn't sure if he liked the heightened emotions she brought out in him. They were a mix of protectiveness, concern, and attraction.

Dr. Flynn Andrews was known to be a skilled surgeon. The one patients wanted in the OR. But he lacked a compassionate bedside manner. He didn't like admitting that, but it was the truth and carried over to his personal life.

No one would call him the cuddling type. Even as a child, he remembered only holding his siblings when his parents handed one to him, and even then, he kept them at a distance if he could. As Callie grew, he would hold her hand, crossing the street or in crowds. Even now, the only things he wanted to hold were a scalpel or the other tools used in the OR.

Flynn might smile and compliment a woman's hair or shoes, but he didn't kiss their hands, not even for show like this morning in front of Dr. Idiot. Yet kissing Anna's hand had been the most natural thing in the world. Flynn had wanted to kiss her on the lips. He wanted to make her smile.

He wiped his face as if that could erase the strange thoughts in his head. If he didn't know any better, he would say he was the one with a brain injury.

"Flynn?" Callie asked.

"Anna would be better off, more comfortable, with

someone else."

He sure would be.

"Buck up, big bro," Callie said. "It's only for a couple of days. You admitted your role in her injury."

His chest tightened. He felt like a big enough jerk as it was. "Please don't remind me."

"I won't. But this is nothing compared to you paying her hospital bill."

"Paying is easy." Flynn enjoyed spending money on people like Brecken and Anna, who needed it more than he did. He stared at her front door. "This—"

"Will be good for you."

As if on cue, the door opened. Taryn stood there. "I thought I heard voices. Is there a problem?"

Callie side-eyed him. "Flynn?"

His sister would be the death of him. Add in two sisters-in-law and he probably was a goner. Whether or not he wanted to do this, they wanted him to stay with Anna. As Callie said, it was only for a couple of days. What was the worst thing that could happen? "No problem."

Flynn rolled his suitcase into the house and stopped.

Callie bumped into him.

"What's wrong?" she asked.

"No barking." He glanced around. "Where's Milo?"

"With Anna," Taryn said. "The dog and cats haven't left her since we got home from the hospital."

"So sweet," Callie said. "And the fact you remembered Milo's name is a good sign. I'll show you to the guest bedroom so you can get settled."

"I'm here for two nights max." He said the words for both their sakes but mainly his.

"You should still make yourself comfortable," Taryn said. "You need to rest as much as Anna does."

"He does." Callie grinned. "Come on."

She pointed out the bathroom at the end of the hall. "There's only one. Towels are in the cabinet next to the shower."

The doors were across the hall from each other. One was open.

"The closed door is Anna's room." Callie went into the open one. "This is the guest bedroom. The guests usually being the foster cats who need time on their own before being given free rein. Right now, Anna is fostering two. They seem sweet if a little skittish, so you might not see much of them."

The bright green painted walls reminded him of a spring meadow. Not that he saw those in L.A., but he'd seen photos of them and on TV. A daybed full of colorful throw pillows sat along the far wall. A three-drawer white dresser was positioned under the window and next to a tall cat tree. Cheery yellow curtains with daisies on them matched the quilt on the bed. He could see Anna everywhere in the room.

"What do you think?" Callie asked.

"Nice." Feminine, yes, but not uncomfortably so. "And a bed's a bed."

"Says the man who paid way too much for his mattress."

"It's like sleeping on a cloud." When he was home, which hadn't been often enough. "This will work for a couple of days."

Two days, not that he was counting.

"Raine dropped off lunch on her way to Tea Leaves and Coffee Beans." Callie opened the closet door as if to urge him to unpack. "Margot will bring by dinner tonight."

"I can—"

"You can't cook."

She wasn't wrong. "I was going to say I can order us food. There are plenty of places in Silver Falls."

Summit Ridge would be too far for deliveries. The food would be cold by the time it arrived.

"Let people help." Callie's soft expression reminded him of Mom. "Everyone feels guilty for not sticking around to help Anna clean up after the shower. People usually do, so I'm not sure why that didn't happen."

"Because Anna acted like she had it all under control."

He didn't know Anna Kent well, but she was the ultimate worker bee, and he meant that in the most positive way. That probably explained why Callie could take a long honeymoon or not go in when she didn't feel well without worrying about Wags and Tails. Anna would keep things running smoothly.

Callie nodded. "Still doesn't make it right."

The guilt clinging to him like a foul stench doubled.

"You don't have to tell me that." He rubbed his neck to loosen the tightness. "What are you going to do about Anna not being able to work?"

"I'm not sure. But Anna's trained Mary Jo and Sam how to wash and dry dogs. Mary Jo also knows how to trim nails.

We'll have to reschedule the other appointments, which is what I plan to do after I leave here."

"I meant about Anna's salary."

"I'll keep paying it, even if she runs out of sick leave," Callie answered without any hesitation. "If not for throwing the baby shower, Anna wouldn't have been on that stepladder. She planned the party, covering for me and my morning sickness. What kind of boss or friend would I be if I didn't pay her knowing she doesn't have much buffer money wise because of Snowy's tooth extractions?"

Flynn hugged her. "You're a wonderful friend."

"Anna's a better one. I was so distracted when I met Brandt, I didn't notice that Anna was sad. I only found out Davis broke up with her when I asked her to call him about our window repairs."

Flynn couldn't imagine Anna seeming down about anything. "You're her best friend. Why didn't she tell you?"

Callie sighed. "Anna wanted me to focus on having fun with Brandt. She thought her being dumped might put a damper on things because I would've wanted to spend time with her."

Flynn had misjudged Anna Kent. "I didn't know."

"I didn't tell anyone because I felt like a horrible friend. I was so into my new guy I didn't pay attention to anything else, including Anna. Yet, after I asked, she called Davis about my window, and he offered to fix it for us."

Somehow Flynn had missed this whole side of the story. "Nice of her...and him."

Callie scoffed. "Not really. Davis only did it to get Anna

back, but his ploy didn't work. He wanted to have his cake and eat it, too. She's better off without him. And the right guy is out there for her. Just a matter of time until she meets him."

Davis didn't seem too smart for letting Anna go. Flynn wanted to know more information, but he kept his curiosity at bay. Anna was nothing more than Callie's best friend. He would stay there with her in case she needed help and to rest himself. In the future, they would see each other as fellow godparents—nothing more.

He pushed in his luggage's handle. "I'll get settled."

"I'll see if Anna's lunch is ready." Callie headed toward the door, but then she stopped and faced him. "And Flynn…"

"What?"

"Thanks." She motioned to the room. "This is totally out of your comfort zone, but I appreciate you staying with Anna."

"Anything for you, baby sis." Flynn meant that. He stared at her stomach. "And the little one growing inside you."

Any stress would affect the baby as much as it did her.

"Go do what you have to do." His smile came easily. "I'll be fine."

Of course he would. Flynn had made split-second life and death decisions for years. He could handle taking care of a certain dog groomer. His tiredness was just getting the better of him.

A few minutes later, Taryn and Callie left. Someone had

taken down the banner and lights. The stepladder wasn't where he'd left it. The room had been cleaned. Even the floor had been mopped and the rugs vacuumed.

In the kitchen, lunch was ready to be served. His plate sat on the counter. Another was on a tray. He picked up the latter, carried it to Anna's room, and knocked on the door. No answer. He opened the door slightly and peered in.

She lay asleep with Milo at her feet. Four or maybe five cats surrounded her. Flynn didn't like the one sleeping on her pillow. That was too close to her head.

The walls and décor were various shades of orange from light to neon. The furniture was black. The combo should have given off Halloween vibes, but somehow it worked with the flower-patterned curtains and the geometric shapes on the comforter. "Anna?"

Milo's ears perked. He raised his head. Two cats stretched as if they had not a care and all the time in the world. The others scattered, jumping off and scurrying under the bed. Anna remained sleeping.

She, however, needed to eat.

Flynn approached the bed. "Hey, it's lunchtime."

Anna didn't wake. An ice pack had slipped off her arm.

Milo barked, and the other cats jumped off the bed.

Finally, Anna stirred. She opened her eyes, but she appeared to be trying to focus. Not surprising. Her brain would be foggy while she recovered.

"It's Flynn." He held out the plate. "Raine brought over lunch for you."

Anna tried to sit up and cringed. "Give me a minute."

"I'm not going anywhere." He was still holding on to the tray, or he would have helped her. "Need help? That's why I'm here."

She blinked. "Oh, right. I forgot you're staying here."

"That's normal. Forgetting, I mean." He would write down any concussion symptoms she experienced. Her doctor might want to know that. "You just woke up. Hungry?"

Anna eyed the plate. "The sandwich looks good."

Someone had cut them into smaller pieces to make it easier for Anna to eat one-handed. There was also a sliced apple and chips. "Wish I could take credit, but your friends have a meal train going after Callie told them I can't cook."

Anna half-laughed. "Is that true?"

"I can cook for myself if need be."

"But you cook as little as possible."

"How did you know that?"

"Lucky guess." The corners of her mouth tilted upward, but the movement appeared to take effort. "You can set the tray on the bed."

"What about the animals?"

Anna looked at her dog. "Milo, off."

Milo appeared to pout if a dog could do that.

"Not today, boy." The dog jumped off the bed. She scooted up into a more reclining position. "I'm not in the mood to keep him away from my food."

"Your head must still hurt."

"I keep waiting for it to stop, but that might take time."

Her frustration made Flynn want to make it better. But brain injuries took time. "You'll get there."

"I'll keep telling myself that."

"A positive attitude helps. I've read studies." As he reached over her to avoid her splinted hand, his palm brushed the comforter covering her. His grip loosened, and he nearly dropped the tray. What was wrong with him? He tightened his fingers. "Sorry."

"No reason to apologize. We don't know each other that well. And that's awkward. Who am I kidding? This would be awkward with Callie. Your being thrown into a caretaker role is awkward for both of us."

"I'm a doctor. By definition, we give care."

"At a hospital or office, right? Not someone's home."

Their gazes met and held.

Flynn didn't know for how long, but he still had the tray. He placed it on the right side of her.

"Thanks. Have you eaten?" she asked.

"Not yet. Taryn and Callie left me a plate in a kitchen."

"You can bring your lunch in here if you don't want to eat alone."

That sounded tempting, but his feelings about Anna ran hot and cold for reasons he didn't understand. He didn't want to delve deeper. Besides, she was being kind given the circumstances. "Thanks, but I'm not hungry yet. Do you need anything else?"

She glanced at the nightstand. A full water bottle sat next to the lamp and a box of tissues. "I'm good, thanks."

Flynn should leave so she could eat, yet his feet remained in place as if glued to the floor. "Do the animals need to eat?"

"Nope." Anna picked up a potato chip. "I only feed them at night and in the morning. I don't have time to run home when I'm at work."

"Makes sense."

"Don't worry about them. They'll let you know when it's mealtime or I can do it."

He wasn't letting her do anything he could do for her. "I don't mind. Though I've never fed a dog or a cat before."

"Easy-peasy."

"You sound like Taryn."

"If only I baked like her…"

They both laughed.

"I don't always take direction well," he admitted. "But I'm sure feeding isn't brain surgery."

"No fellowship or board certification required."

He laughed again. Callie must have spouted off his background to Anna in the past.

Anna's gaze softened, not from being unfocused. This seemed to be something different.

"I know this isn't what you planned on doing when you came to Silver Falls for some R&R." She took a breath as if talking exerted her. "But you're making life easier on my friends, who have businesses to run. I'm sure they appreciate it, and I do too. I'll try not to be a burden."

Her words sounded like an apology. He didn't like that when he was responsible for her injury. "A burden is the last thing you could be."

She raised an eyebrow. "You didn't always think that way. What's changed?"

143

"I didn't know you. And your dog left an impression that colored my judgment. Besides, being here is the least I can do considering…"

"What happened was an accident."

"But—"

"An accident means no one's fault, including yours." She sounded sincere, and her expression held no ill will. "You keep blaming yourself. Please stop. I accepted your apology. Let's move on."

She didn't hold him responsible. The relief was palpable, but he needed to make sure. "You mean that?"

"Why wouldn't I?"

"I…" Words failed him.

"Go eat and then rest, Dr. Andrews. Dog groomer's orders."

"I'm here to look after you," he shot back. "And you don't have to call me Doctor."

"You need your rest as much as me. Maybe more." She smiled softly, and his pulse shot up. "Calling you Doctor got your attention, right, Flynn?"

As his name rolled off her tongue, flutters filled his stomach. The urge to tug on his collar returned. He must have gone too long without a date because he was reacting like a teenager.

"If I need anything, I'll let you know," she continued. "After I eat, I plan to take another nap. You should do the same. If Milo wants out, he'll let one of us know."

Flynn had been so captivated by Anna he'd forgotten about the dog or the cats or anything else.

Milo sat on the floor next to the bed, staring at Anna as if the sun rose and set on her. In the dog's world, it did.

"Go," she urged. "And remember to eat when you're hungry."

Except Flynn still didn't want to leave her, which told him to get away from her now. As he walked to the door, he glanced over his shoulder.

His gaze met hers, and his heart collided against his chest. His breath stilled until he forced himself to breathe. Something—awareness or attraction—pulsed through him. What was going on?

Chapter Twelve

DAYLIGHT SHONE THROUGH the cracks in the blinds, which told Anna she hadn't napped for long after lunch. The ice pack was no longer there, and her arm hurt. Her head didn't feel much better.

It wasn't only the pain.

She felt…off.

But in other ways things were completely normal.

The cats purred beside her. The frequency of their purrs would help heal her arm if she'd fractured it, but her fingers moved just fine without any pain. She didn't want to complain, especially to Flynn.

The lunch tray no longer sat on the bed. Flynn must have picked it up while she slept. She grimaced. No doubt her mouth had been hanging open. Had she been snoring?

Nope. She didn't want to know.

So what if he saw me like that?

Flynn was a doctor. He saw patients in all sorts of strange states, awake and asleep. Except a few times, not many, the way he looked at her didn't seem professional or friendly. As in *friend* friend. It hadn't been flirtatious, but there'd been some heat. Okay, more like a spark, but she'd glimpsed interest and…

Better not go there.

Brain injury. That explained her weird thoughts about him. Her mind wasn't fully functioning normally. The feelings she'd experienced when he brought over pizza must be complicating her jumbled gray matter.

Whatever the reason, Flynn was nothing more than her best friend's older brother who happened to be a doctor. That fact and his misplaced guilt were the only reasons he was with her.

Easy-peasy, right?

Even if Anna wanted to think about him as anything else, nothing would happen between them. She wasn't one for casual relationships with a known expiration date. The first part was why she hadn't wanted to date Davis nonexclusively when he wanted to get back together. Besides, everyone she knew believed Pippa was the woman for Flynn. Even Anna agreed, albeit more reluctantly now than before. But he'd been so kind to her at the hospital.

No matter.

If things worked out as she hoped, Flynn would leave tomorrow. Twenty-four hours from now, give or take a few. That would be forty-eight hours from when she hit her head. The doctor—she couldn't remember his name—mentioned a longer timeframe, but when Flynn stepped out to talk to his mom, Anna had asked the nurse to clarify that part of the discharge instructions and circle the time so she didn't forget it.

But first things first.

Anna needed to go to the bathroom. She wasn't at the cross-her-legs-and-squirm stage, but she didn't want to find herself there. The bedroom door was ajar. The bathroom was close. She could travel the short trek to the toilet alone. All she needed to do was stand.

Anna scooted to the side of her bed.

Pumpkin, her orange boy, meowed.

"Where did everyone go?" No other cats were in sight. They might be with Milo. Though Inky and Midge still seemed skittish about this place and about Milo. They might be under the bed, the couch, or a chair. They came out when they wanted attention or food. She didn't worry about them escaping the house because Flynn probably wouldn't leave her alone. The guy had responsible written all over him, whether in the arrogant doctor or the overprotective big brother mode.

As she sat, a frisson of worry kept her from standing. People had helped her since her fall, but she could do this on her own. Standing took little skill, only some balance and hers was improving by the hour.

I can do this.

With a deep inhalation, Anna placed her hands on the mattress, one on each side of her, and stood.

The room didn't tilt or sway. Thank goodness. Now to get to the bathroom. With no stairs to negotiate, she only had to make a left turn and avoid any fur babies that might plop to the floor. Sometimes, the cats did that when she carried the laundry basket.

Paws sounded against the hardwood floor. Milo pranced

into the room with a squeaky toy shaped like a newspaper in his mouth.

Her heart swelled with love. "Aren't you the cutest?"

He dropped the toy, sat, and stared at her expectantly.

She knew what he wanted, but… "I'd love to play fetch but bending over wouldn't be a good idea. Mommy has to go to the bathroom."

Milo panted.

"You can come with me as long as you go first, okay?"

Milo's tail wagged, but he remained seated.

"Stay there."

Better get going.

"What are you doing?" Flynn stood in the doorway. He wasn't smiling, yet his mussed hair looked as if he'd been sleeping. Surprisingly, his grumpy expression and adorable sleep-rumpled hair worked well together. "Anna?"

Oh, right. He'd asked her a question before she went all boy band fangirl on him. She raised her chin slowly. Anything involving movement had to be slow. "Going to the bathroom."

"By yourself?"

"Milo's coming with me."

The dog barked.

She cringed at the sharp sound.

Flynn's mouth quirked. "I'm sure he'll be a big help if you fall."

Anna couldn't tell whether he was trying to be funny. "I don't need help using the bathroom."

A beat passed. And another. "I'm sure you don't. But

you might need some help getting there."

"Maybe." Standing made her tired. She didn't want to be stupid about this—about her health. Still… "You should be able to go back to Margot's tomorrow."

"Maybe."

"I'm getting better."

"You're better than you were, but head injuries are fickle. Let's see how you do the rest of the day before making future plans."

Anna wished he didn't sound so reasonable.

As Flynn walked toward her, he glanced at the dog. "Let's help her get to the bathroom. You can go in, and I'll stand watch outside."

Milo stood.

At least they were getting along better, considering Flynn's first impression of Milo. Maybe he needed a dog. A dog would give him something to come home to rather than spend his nights at the hospital, which according to Callie, he did far too often. Though a dog took work and commitment and couldn't be left alone for that long. There were doggy daycares all over Southern California, but that might not be the best situation.

Now a cat…

A cat could be left alone and not mind. Two cats might be perfect companions for him. Two cats like Inky and Midge, though getting them to L.A. might be an issue. Still, the rescue had transported animals to forever homes in the past.

Flynn reached out with his right hand. "I'll be behind

you. If you fall, I don't want to chance hurting your left arm more."

Since he didn't plan on going into the bathroom with her, she would do things his way. The cats could be discussed later. "Sure."

Anna placed her palm against him. Something sparked. She jerked her arm away.

"Static electricity. Sorry," he said.

She tried again. No shock, but his skin was electric-blanket warm.

The heat felt good. Better than it should.

His fingers wrapped around hers. The sight of their linked hands shouldn't appeal to her as much as it did.

"See if you can take a step."

His voice—albeit soft—jolted her back to reality. With a steadying breath, she moved her right foot and promptly tilted forward.

Flynn caught her. "I've got you."

Boy, did he. Her face pressed against his chest, and he smelled oh so good. She wasn't sure if it was his detergent or him, but she wouldn't mind another sniff.

"You okay?" he asked.

Oops. No sniffing, but she inhaled quickly. If not for Flynn, she would be flat on her face or bottom. Neither would be good. She might need some help. "Yep. Thanks."

"Feeling steady?"

His heartbeat was steady and a little fast. But that wasn't what he meant. She straightened. No wobbling. "Yes."

"Try another step."

Anna did. She never expected walking to bring a sense of pride, but it did. Her idea of being on her own by tomorrow, however, seemed like a pipe dream now.

"Out of the way, Milo," Flynn ordered.

Whoa. The dog moved into the hallway. It usually took a time or two for him to obey her. "He listened."

"Yes, I told him to keep an eye on the cats, and he's decided he's a herding dog. No nipping, but he's kept them in the living room except for the orange one."

"Pumpkin. That's his name."

"Fitting. He strutted away with his tail in the air and more attitude than a new cohort of surgical residents." Flynn's warm breath sent goose bumps trailing along her skin. "The two black cats…"

"Inky and Midge. They're fosters. A bonded pair."

"A what?"

"Cats who have a special attachment. They aren't related, but they're besties who do better together, so they'll be adopted as a package deal."

"Well, the pair fell right in line as if Milo was the Pied Piper of felines. The gray one and the white one…"

"Bristol and Snowy."

"They took more convincing." Slowly, with him behind her, she made her way to the doorway. "You're doing great."

"Bet you say that to all the patients."

"Only the ones I like."

Anna laughed. She stumbled, but Flynn had hold of her, so she didn't fall. "Your arrogant side is showing, Doctor, but thanks for catching me."

He helped her take another step. "You've got this."

She hoped so because head injury or not, having someone take care of her, if only out of obligation or guilt, pushed all her buttons. It couldn't become a habit or be more than tonight.

"Almost there." She said the words for her own sake. "But I don't think Milo should go in. I'm not as steady on my feet as I thought I'd be."

As I hoped I'd be. Admitting that was hard. She wanted to be better. Not tomorrow or in a week or six weeks. Now.

"Probably a good idea." He positioned her so she stood with her right side next to the counter but kept hold of her. "Ready for me to let go?"

No! Anna hoped she hadn't spoken the word aloud. He hadn't reacted so she must not have. Thank goodness. "Yes. I'm ready."

So, so ready.

Flynn placed her hand on the counter, but he didn't let go of her. "Use this to keep your balance but mind the sink."

"I will."

"I'll close the door once you're out of the way, but please don't lock it in case you fall."

Anna tried to imagine something worse than falling off the toilet with her pants around her ankles. Nothing came to mind unless she wet her pants, which might happen if this took much longer. She muttered a prayer that neither scenario came to pass. "Okay."

He let go of her but stayed close. "You're standing on your own."

Standing and not falling. She would cheer, but that might upset her balance.

With her hand gripping the edge of the counter like a lifeline, she took a hesitant step and then another.

"Looking good," Flynn cheered.

Milo barked.

She continued slowly until she reached the end of the counter and stopped. The toilet was right there, and she'd never been as happy to see the seat cover up as she was then. Not that she ever put it down, but Flynn might have. "I'm good."

As soon as Flynn closed the door, Anna leaned her hip against the counter. She shouldn't be worn out from a short walk, but she was. Still, she didn't want to take too long.

Pulling down her sleep pants was easy enough, but sitting would be tricky since her left hand, which was closest to the counter, couldn't hold on to anything. The shower curtain wouldn't be much support.

Maybe if she rested her arm on the counter.

She tried that.

Talk about awkward. She nearly fell over, but her bottom hit the seat. "Yes!"

Her own voice made her flinch.

"Need help?" He kept his voice low.

"No." Anna did her business, flushed the toilet, and pulled up her pants as far as they would go with her seated. She stood to get the pants up over her hips. They were barely in place when the bathroom tilted. She closed her eyes and then opened them.

Okay, better.

She stood at the sink and washed her good hand. As she reached for the towel, the bathroom spun. She grabbed onto the counter, but her wet hand slid and… "Flynn!"

Milo barked.

A gush of air skittered across her skin. Arms circled her waist and held her upright. "Are you hurt?"

"Dizzy." She closed her eyes. It didn't help.

"I won't let you fall. Your hand is wet."

"I was trying to dry it and…"

Flynn picked her up. "Let's get you to your room."

She was afraid to open her eyes. "You'll hurt your back carrying me."

"It's fine."

"No." She wasn't thin like Pippa. Anna enjoyed food, especially desserts, too much. Her drink orders at Raine's place wouldn't be considered low-calorie or healthy. "I'm—"

"Perfect the way you are. Well, minus the concussion and splint?"

Her chest tightened. The backs of her eyelids burned until her eyes watered.

Flynn set her onto the bed. "You're crying. Do you hurt that badly?"

Anna kept her eyes closed. It wasn't the dizziness. "No."

The mattress depressed next to her. Flynn must have sat. He moved hair off her forehead.

That only brought more tears.

"What is it?" His voice was tender.

For a moment, in the depths of her injured brain, she

imagined he cared about her because to him she was still perfect even with her flaws and foibles and the family-in-name-only she'd left behind.

Anna sniffled. "You're being so nice to me."

"Want me to insult you or one of your animals so you'll stop crying?"

"Not really." She cracked open her eyes. Things moved like she was aboard a ship, but only in small waves, not a stormy sea.

He wiped away her tears with his thumb. "Better?"

"Yes." Her voice cracked.

"Let's give your stomach time to settle down before you drink more water."

She didn't trust what the motion might do to her head so didn't want to nod. "Okay."

"Do you need anything?"

You. Except that wasn't the right answer.

The doorbell rang.

Milo barked as if intruders were trying to knock down the front door with a battering ram.

She covered her right ear with her hand and raised her left shoulder as much as she could to block her left ear.

He stood. "I'll answer the door and try to quiet Milo."

Flynn left the room before she had a chance to reply. She missed having him close to her. And that…

Was a problem.

Warning lights blared in her aching head. She couldn't fall for Flynn. People fell for their caretakers in books and movies, but that wasn't allowed. Not in real life—her life.

These odd feelings stemmed from her injuries and loneliness. She'd been lonely for nearly sixteen months now. Her situation was pushing her to the extreme. All she had to do was remember that.

And not forget Flynn was being nice to her because of Callie and his family. If he wanted a relationship, he would be with Pippa, who was more a doctor's wife type than Anna could ever hope to be. But he didn't want a relationship. He wasn't that different from Davis. Something else Anna needed to remember—concussion or not.

Chapter Thirteen

A S FLYNN HURRIED to the front door, he tried to slow his racing pulse. He was there to help Anna, not crush on her. And him even thinking the word *crush* was a massive problem.

Milo barked as if a big brown truck had pulled in front of the house with a delivery of dog treats.

"Quiet." Flynn didn't want Anna's head to hurt more. "It's probably Margot with dinner."

Milo stopped barking and panted. Maybe the dog wasn't that bad.

Flynn opened the door. Margot stood on the welcome mat with a large bag. "Thought it might be you. Come in."

He followed Margot into the kitchen where she set her bag on the counter and preheated the oven. "Anna enjoys Italian food, so I brought lasagna, a salad, and garlic bread." Margot winked. "Figured that way, you'd know I'm not playing matchmaker. And there's enough for leftovers."

"I appreciate that."

"Thought you might also want to know Pippa may have set up a new dating profile, but she hasn't gone out with anyone. In case you have a change of heart about our town's favorite florist."

"Good to know."

Margot perked up. "Really."

The woman was incorrigible. "No."

She wagged her finger at Flynn. "Don't raise a woman's hopes, Dr. Andrews."

"Will you ever stop playing Cupid?"

Her blue eyes twinkled. "Never. You'll change your mind about a relationship, and Pippa will be waiting when you do."

"If you say so."

"I do." Margot rubbed her palms together. "Oh, and I believe I've found the perfect match for our Anna."

His throat tightened. "Anna Kent?"

Margot's hands flew to her hips. "How many Annas do you know in Silver Falls?"

"One, but I wanted to make sure I hadn't missed any."

"Well, it turns out Dr. Wingate is single, and Summit Ridge isn't that far away. Since she's been released to her primary care physician, there shouldn't be any issue with her being his patient."

True, but no way. Doctor Idiot didn't deserve someone as special as Anna. "Why him?"

Margot's blue eyes twinkled. "Doctor Wingate is a sharp guy. He caught on fast that you weren't Anna's serious boyfriend or even dating."

Flynn rocked back on his heels. "How did he know?"

"Said you were too clinical with your questions and kept your distance. Most guys want to hold their girlfriends and get into bed with them, even if it's not good for a patient."

"I'm a doctor. I wouldn't do that." Even if Flynn had wanted to hold her.

"That's what Dr. Wingate told me. Though he said this morning you almost had him convinced, but Anna wasn't into it."

Yeah, she'd been confused, and Flynn had hated not being able to say why he'd acted so lovey-dovey.

"But the fact Dr. Wingate let you stay overnight with her tells me he's a good guy. Exactly what our Anna needs."

Not ours.

His Anna.

Wait. Where did that come from? Flynn gulped.

"After Anna's had time to heal, I'll invite them both over to dinner, and voilà. Maybe we'll have another Christmas wedding."

Flynn's stomach dropped. "That's only eight months from now."

"Neither are fresh out of college," Margot explained. "Anna will be thirty-two. Dr. Wingate must be in his late twenties or early thirties. Once you know, you know."

"I don't see the two of them together. He's too…"

"What?"

"Frat boy. Bro dude."

"Well, he loves animals and could tell Anna was special."

"Tell how? She's concussed."

"You'll see." Margot unpacked her bag. "That gives me an idea. You and Pippa should double-date with them. Then you'll see I'm never wrong about these things."

He side-eyed her.

Margot held up her hands. "What? Pippa would make a perfect doctor's wife."

"This isn't the 1950s."

"You know what I mean about Pippa." The oven beeped. Margot slid the casserole pan and a foil-covered loaf of bread into the oven. "This will keep things warm until you're ready to eat."

He needed to stop the matchmaking. "Pippa's life is here."

The same as Anna's. Why was he having this discussion?

Margot placed a salad in the refrigerator. "There are hospitals in Washington State. Summit Ridge isn't a level-one trauma center, but skilled surgeons are needed everywhere."

She'd put too much thought into this. He'd better change the subject. "Did you bring dessert?"

"Homemade cookies." Margot pulled out a lidded plastic container. "Enough to last a few days."

"Thanks, but I'm not sure how long I'll be here." He peered around the corner to the hallway. The door was open. "Anna thinks she'll be fine on her own tomorrow."

"Optimism will keep her going, but I don't think that will happen."

Margot was at the hub of Silver Falls rumors. He didn't want Anna's dizzy spell in the bathroom discussed over coffee at Raine's place. "Neither do I. Time will tell."

"Yes, it will."

Margot folded her bag. "Taryn's in charge of breakfast tomorrow. She or Garrett will be by in the morning. Pippa will drop off lunch. Beth is having dinner delivered."

"Thank you."

"Thank Sam," Margot said to his surprise. "He's the one who came up with the idea and set up the meal train online. He didn't give Callie the link since she needs to rest. Just told her Anna's meals were covered and not to worry about her oldest brother's lack of cooking skills."

"I can cook when I want to."

"Which isn't often." Margot laughed. "Call if you need anything. Angus and Sadie miss you. Your room is there for you when you need it."

"Do you want to see Anna?"

"Let her rest." Margot tucked the folded bag under her arm. "I'll be back in a couple of days with another meal. You might not be here, but she needs to eat and shouldn't worry about meals, even though she cooks whether she wants to or not."

If Margot planned her dig to be subtle, she'd failed, but he would let it slide. Anna had told him she cooked most nights.

Margot petted the dog. "Take care of everyone, Milo."

Milo barked.

"Be sure to take care of yourself," Margot said to Flynn. "You won't do your patient any good if you don't."

"Anna's not my patient." The words catapulted out. If she were his patient, he would need to drop the case immediately. He was too close. "I mean…"

"I meant in general terms." As Margot headed to the front door, she glanced over her shoulder and smiled. "Rest.

I'm sure you didn't sleep well last night."

The door opened and closed.

Milo stared at Flynn. "It's not time for dinner yet."

The dog tilted his head.

"You went out back."

The dog turned his head the other way.

"Don't worry about what Margot said. Doctor Idiot isn't anyone you have to worry about. He looks like a popped-collar, fancy-watch-wearing dude. Not Anna's…your mom's type."

Which meant Flynn wasn't her type, either.

"The guy might be perfect for Pippa." On paper and on Flynn's arm, she seemed perfect for him. But there'd been no real spark. No flutters or heat. Not like there was with…

"Flynn?" Anna asked.

Adrenaline surged as if he'd been paged for a code blue. He ran to the room with Milo at his heels and found Anna in bed with the five cats. "What's wrong?"

His voice must have been loud because she winced, and the cats scattered off the bed and out of the room.

"Sorry." She looked half-asleep. Her eyelids fluttered. "I knocked over my water bottle. It has a lid, but some water might have spilled."

A few drops had fallen from the straw onto the floor.

It wasn't an emergency. She was okay.

Relief flowed through him. He'd thought…

Flynn didn't know what he'd thought except he didn't want anything to happen to Anna.

One breath. Two breaths. His pulse settled.

"You okay?" she asked.

"Fine." The word came out harsher than he intended. He grabbed a tissue from the box on the nightstand, wiped up the water, and placed the cup back where it belonged.

"Bet they don't make surgeons clean up after they operate."

"Only ourselves."

"I don't mind cleaning. It gives me a sense of accomplishment. After some of the places I lived..."

That piqued his interest. "Around here?"

"No, in Cali. Not the best places for a kid. But I love where I live now."

He'd learned more about her past. Not much, but that was okay. For now. "You keep this place nice and tidy. Did you decorate it?"

"I did. I didn't have enough for the safety deposit as well as first and last month's rent, so my landlord offered me a sweat equity deal. It's worked out for both of us."

"Sounds like it." Flynn had no idea how long she'd been there, but the painting and work wasn't new. He didn't know how much a dog groomer earned, which might be why she worried about the hospital bill last night. "It's nice your landlord worked with you."

"I met her through the local animal rescue. I volunteer there. I also groom her animals. No charge, of course."

"Of course." The more he learned about Anna the more she impressed him. "How did you get into dog grooming?"

Anna reached for the water bottle, raised her head slightly, and sipped. "It's kind of a long story."

Flynn didn't want to push. "Later, then."

Relief flooded her expression.

Must be some story. "Margot dropped off dinner. Lasagna, salad, garlic bread, and cookies."

"Sounds delicious."

Anna hadn't eaten much for lunch. He hoped she had an appetite now. "Hungry?"

"I could eat."

"It's warming in the oven."

She pushed herself upright.

"Oh, no, you don't." He fought the urge to touch her shoulders and pointed to her pillow instead. "I may not be the greatest cook in the world, but I can plate food with the best of them."

She lay down. "Guess those scalpel skills come in handy outside of the OR."

He laughed. "Sometimes. I'll get dinner ready."

"Would you…" Her voice trailed off.

Flynn stepped closer to the edge of the bed. "What?"

"Would you eat dinner in here with me?" The hope in her eyes matched the expression on her face.

His heart rate took off as if he'd floored his car's accelerator.

She looked away. "If you'd rather not…"

"I'd be happy to eat dinner in here."

Her gaze jerked up to meet his. "You would?"

He smiled at her. "I would. Do you need to use the bathroom before?"

"No."

"It's been a while since you were light-headed. Stay hydrated."

"I am." As if to emphasize the point, she sipped. "I was thirsty. That's why I ended up knocking it over."

"Okay." At some point she'd need to make another trip, unless she wanted to wait to brush her teeth after dinner. "I'll be right back."

"Could you help me sit?" She stared up at him through her eyelashes. "I can't eat lying down."

No, she couldn't. He moved closer. "Let's go slow in case you get dizzy."

"Okay."

The closer he got, the more he could smell her sunshine and sugar scent. She hadn't showered, and he saw no lotion on the nightstand. Unless she'd put some perfume on in the bathroom earlier, but he hadn't noticed the scent before.

"Flynn?" she asked.

"Figuring out the safest way to do this." Liar, though safety was his priority with her. Not only her, everyone. "I'm putting my arm around you. Ready?"

"Yes, though I sat by myself earlier."

"You also ended up dizzy in the bathroom. Let's try it my way this time." It didn't take much, and she sat. "I'm tucking pillows behind you."

"Five-star service."

"Only the best for the godmother of my future niece or nephew." Once the pillows were adjusted, he fixed her blanket. "How's that?"

She gazed into his eyes.

Flynn's breath stilled.

Something passed between them. Something he couldn't explain but he felt it inside of him.

"Thank you," she said finally, breaking whatever spell he'd been under.

"I'll be right back with dinner."

"You might want to feed everyone else first, or they'll never let us eat in peace. The instructions for each are in the tall cabinet next to the refrigerator."

"You think of everything."

"When I had to work extra for Callie, Sam helped me out by feeding them."

"Nice kid."

"He'll be an excellent nurse. Though Wags and Tails will miss him."

Anna meant it that she would miss Sam. He knew Callie would, too. It reminded him how Taryn felt about Brecken and Raine about Timmy. "I'm sure. Be right back."

The detailed instructions and measuring cups made feeding easy. Each animal had a specific location for eating. All kept giving him the evil eye until he placed their bowls on the floor.

He opened cabinets and drawers until he found what he needed: oven mitts, a hot pad, serving utensil, plates, napkins, and flatware. He'd washed the tray earlier, so it was ready to use again. Dinner didn't look as social media ready as lunch had, but everything fit on the tray.

He carried their dinner into the bedroom.

"Something smells delicious." Anna's voice sounded

stronger, which was a good sign. So was her having an appetite. "Leave it to Margot. She's such a good cook."

"That's why I stay with her. It's like being at a B and B that serves three restaurant-quality meals a day. Nothing against my family, and while Taryn wins for desserts and Raine for beverages, Margot's the best cook in the bunch."

Anna grabbed a slice of garlic bread off the tray. "I doubt anyone would disagree. Now her matchmaking abilities…"

"Brandt tells her to stop, but my family seems happy with the results."

She lowered the half-eaten slice of bread. "Are you?"

"I love my in-laws." Flynn laughed. "A year and a half ago when we were all single, I would've never expected to say that, but now, I can."

"You're next."

"I was next as soon as Keaton asked Raine to marry him."

Anna bypassed the salad and scooped a forkful of lasagna. "Does it bother you?"

"No, because Margot can try but she won't succeed."

Anna laughed and took a bite. "So good."

He took a bite of lasagna. It was mouthwateringly good with the right amount of tang from the Italian sausage and blend of spices. The tomato sauce complemented the cheeses.

"I've known Margot since I moved to town. She won't give up on a cause."

"She has her heart set on me and…"

"Pippa."

Huh? Anna didn't sound upset about that. "She brought up Pippa when she was here."

"Pippa's great. I mean, you wouldn't find someone more suitable."

"If I were looking for a girlfriend, maybe. But I'm not. And suitable isn't everything."

"Yeah, right." Anna ate more.

Flynn sipped a cup of flavored mineral water. "What's that supposed to mean?"

"Dating or falling in love with someone suitable is important to men."

"A few."

"Try many."

Another story. This one he wanted to hear. He scooped up more lasagna. "Any in Silver Falls?"

"Summit Ridge."

That was more information than Flynn expected to hear. He had a feeling he knew who. "That Davis guy."

Anna's lips parted. "How do you know about him?"

"Callie mentioned the name."

"Davis and I dated the December before last." Anna picked at another slice of garlic bread. "I thought the relationship was going well, but he thought I was too clingy, so he broke up with me."

"You don't seem like the clingy type."

She shrugged. "It was almost Christmas, and I didn't want to be alone for another holiday."

Another hung in the air between them. No one should be alone for any Christmas.

She ate another bite of bread. "I enjoyed being with him. He kept asking me out, so I said yes. I opened up and told him things I rarely mention to anyone else. I thought there was something more between us. If that's clingy, then I suppose I was."

The guy had to be stupid for thinking Anna was clingy. It also made sense why she didn't open up to more people. "I'm sorry that happened."

"It wasn't meant to be." She stared at her plate. "He wanted to get back together, but only if we saw other people. He wasn't ready to date exclusively. That felt like a step backward from where we'd been, so I said no."

"Any regrets?"

"None. He doesn't, either. The next woman he asked out he married. Even contractors know what they consider a suitable date or spouse."

"You're suitable." Flynn spoke without even thinking. "You have a great home, a good job, pets, and friends."

"Yes, but…"

"What?"

She lowered her fork. It clattered against her plate. "No family."

"Do you want to talk about them?"

She shrugged. "My parents were drug addicts. I guess they might have been decent humans at one point, but I don't remember that. I do remember them strung out, being evicted multiple times, living in places I wouldn't let my pets into, and hanging around very sketchy people. I had to fend for myself a lot and did okay, until I overhead them saying they needed to sell me to afford more drugs. I ran away that night. I ended up in the foster care system until I graduated high school. But I graduated, which is better than what might have happened to me if I'd stayed."

The air rushed from his lungs. Callie had warned him, but this wasn't the past he'd imagined. He had a feeling there was more that happened between running away and the foster system. "I'm glad you escaped that life."

"Me too. I can tell by your expression you're shocked. Most people are."

"Your parents…"

"My mom ended up OD'ing. She'd done it before when I was with them, but that time killed her. My dad's in jail. But they stopped being my parents long before that happened."

"I'm so sorry."

"It happens. Unfortunately." She sounded more resigned than upset. "The reason the background check couldn't find anything about me was I had help getting a new name. Someday, my father will get out of prison. I doubt he'd try to find me, but this way he can't."

"And your new name?"

"My last foster family was nice. They might have adopted me had I been placed with them when I was younger, but they knew I wanted to get away, so they had a friend, who was in the government or something. His name was Kent."

"And Anna."

She blushed. "Ever see the movie *Freaky Friday*?"

"A long time ago."

"The lead character's first name was Anna. I loved that movie."

"So Anna Kent."

She nodded. "Kent knew a friend of a friend who owned a kennel and grooming shop near Seattle. He found me a job there. My foster family paid for a one-way plane ticket."

Flynn had to ask. "You told Davis this."

"Only about my parents. I was squirming, and he looked upset. He broke up with me the next day."

"Loser."

She laughed. "Thanks. Him calling me clingy must have been an excuse. I don't blame him. Addiction can be genetic, right?"

"You don't need to justify Davis's mistake. And it was a big one." Flynn hated that the man had hurt Anna over a past and parents she had no control over. "People can be predisposed to addiction, but it's not a given you will be."

"I don't drink much, and the only pain meds I've ever had were at the hospital. Why risk it?" She ate more of the lasagna. "This is really tasty."

"It is." She was changing the subject, and he would let her. But his respect for her had skyrocketed. "There's salad."

"I eat that last. I read somewhere the French do. Helps with digestion or something."

Flynn wanted to take her to Paris and let her eat like the French ate. Who was he kidding?

He wanted to give her all the things she'd only read or dreamed about. He wanted to make sure she never stopped smiling. He wanted to make her life better.

"Please educate me." Flynn scooted closer to Anna. "Do we eat Margot's homemade cookies before the salad or after them?"

Chapter Fourteen

AFTER DINNER, ANNA slid into bed with Flynn hovering over her. She understood what Callie had meant about her brothers, especially the oldest, being overprotective. But unlike Callie, Anna didn't think it sucked. She enjoyed the attention. He would keep her safe. That hadn't always been the case with the men in her life. She appreciated that in him.

Flynn had helped her to the bathroom, and that visit went better than the other. No dizziness, only strange flutters in her stomach resembling butterflies. She'd brushed her teeth and felt almost human again. Talk about a good feeling.

A shower would help. Her hair needed to be washed, but she would do that herself. Not tonight. She was too tired with aches and pains and weird thoughts. So many of those.

"Milo's outside. I'll let him inside so he can be with you." Flynn adjusted her covers. He was careful to avoid her arm and not to jostle her. "Need anything?"

Anna was tempted to ask him to stay until she fell asleep. Even though she wasn't one hundred percent there mentally, that would be too much to ask of Flynn.

"I'm good." She was overall. He'd taken care of her today as had her friends who dropped off food. Though she must be more out of it than she realized to have shared her past with Flynn. Who was she kidding? She'd told him for only one reason—to push him away. Nothing else made sense. Only he hadn't reacted as she expected. Flynn hadn't cringed and stared at her as if she were a stranger like Davis had. If anything, telling Flynn seemed to bring them closer, which shocked her.

"I'll leave the door cracked so the animals can come in and out." He stood above her with an unreadable expression. "Let me know if you need anything."

"I will."

Flynn had been supportive and kind tonight. He'd almost looked angry as she'd told him about her parents and Davis. Something else she hadn't expected but appreciated.

"Thanks," she added.

"You're welcome." He kissed her right cheek, the one part of her head that didn't hurt. "Sleep well."

Anna hated when he stood, taking his warmth and scent away. She fought the urge to touch the spot where he'd kissed her. Dr. Flynn Andrews kept surprising her in good ways. She might even be developing a slight crush. "You, too."

They locked gazes once again. If she didn't have a concussion, she might analyze it. But the reason didn't matter. She was grateful for his help. If she looked too deeply, she might realize he was only being nice, and for today, she preferred daydreaming, even if nothing more would happen.

She got comfortable in bed.

One by one, the cats joined her. Bristol lay against her right leg. Snowy took her left. Pumpkin jumped onto Anna's pillow.

"Oh no, you don't." Flynn picked up the orange cat and placed him on the pillow next to hers. "Not tonight, Pumpkin. Maybe tomorrow."

Midge and Inky searched for a place.

"Half the bed's open if you want it." He scratched under Midge's neck. The black cat rubbed against his hand as if that would get her more attention.

"For someone who doesn't have any pets, you've got the touch." Anna had spent days coaxing the foster cats out from under the bed. "Midge and Inky are people-shy, but they've warmed right up to you."

He flashed a lopsided grin. "I may have given them extra treats."

That didn't surprise her. "So that's your secret."

"Why do you think I offered you more of Margot's cookies?" He winked. "Treats are the perfect softener. When I did my pediatrics rotation, we gave the kids stickers."

"Smart." Anna didn't want to be attracted to him, but she was. "Do I need softening?"

"No," he said without missing a beat. "But a little spoiling when you're injured never hurts."

It didn't in her case. "You're good at spoiling."

But his words only confirmed what she'd thought. He was being nice because of her situation. Anything else was only in her imagination.

That was okay. Flynn was showing her what she could have someday if she remained patient and didn't try to force more to happen. Good guys existed. The one for her was out there somewhere. "Does this mean you put away your arrogant side, Doctor?"

"For now." Laughter danced in his eyes. "As soon as you feel better, the arrogance will return."

Anna laughed, but she was torn. She wanted to feel better, but she hoped Flynn stuck around another day or two. She didn't need to be spoiled, but she enjoyed his company. Dinner tonight had been fun, much better than eating alone, even when the conversation turned heavy. "Well, good night, nice-guy surgeon."

"Most men don't consider being called a nice guy a compliment."

"You're not like most men."

"I won't disagree with that." Once again, he sounded amused.

When Flynn reached the doorway, he glanced back. Their gazes locked once again. His closed-mouth smile made her breath catch.

It's nothing.

Even if it felt like a big something.

All in my head.

Tomorrow things, including her mind, would be clearer. At least she hoped so.

SHE WAS FALLING.

She kept falling and falling into darkness and the cold.
So cold.

Goose bumps covered her skin. The chill went all the way to her bones. And she continued to fall.

Down. Down. Down.

Help me. Please help me.

Anna screamed. She opened her eyes. It was still dark. "Flynn!"

The word burst from her lips. She struggled to catch her breath.

"I'm here." He sat on the bed with his hands lightly against each of her shoulders. "You had a bad dream. I didn't want you to thrash around. If it had gotten worse, I would have woken you."

"I was falling, only I didn't hit the ground. I kept falling into nothingness."

He rubbed her right arm. "That must've been scary."

She shivered. "It was."

As her eyes adjusted to the darkness, Flynn came into focus. His hair was a mess. A shadow covered his lower face—stubble. And he wore sleep pants, no shirt.

She swallowed. "Sorry, I woke you."

"Don't apologize." He yawned. "You've been through a lot."

So had he with not resting enough. "You need to sleep, too."

His fingers rubbed circles on her shoulder. "Plenty of time for that. The cats and Milo took off."

"They'll be back."

He leaned closer, so close his warm breath was on her neck. "Have nightmares often?"

"Occasionally." Whenever she thought about her past. Anna didn't want to know what that meant subconsciously. She wanted to forget about her life in California. "It's no big deal. I just need a little time to let my pulse and mind settle."

Anna would have turned on the light, except her head might hurt more.

"Will you be able go back to sleep?" he asked in such a gentle voice she wanted to throw herself against him and not let go.

She also didn't want to lie to him. "I don't know. Maybe not right away, but I'll be okay. I'll fall asleep eventually. Go back to bed."

"Doesn't work that way."

"Says who?"

He yawned, only proving the guy was human and tired. "Doctor Arrogant."

She laughed. "You're half-asleep, Doc."

"You'd be amazed what I've accomplished in this state."

Her pulse skittered, but not in the same way it had during the nightmare. Anna didn't know if he'd meant the words to come out as flirty as they had. "I'm fine. Get some rest."

"Not until you fall asleep."

His eyelids looked so droopy. That wasn't good.

"Lie down or you'll fall asleep and land on my arm or something." Her voice came out curt, as if she was getting on Milo after he'd misbehaved, but she was tired and hurting and attracted to Flynn. Not a good combination for her patience. "Please," she added to be nice.

"I won't say no to that offer." He lay on her right side on top of the cover.

At least the bed was queen-sized. Something to be grateful for. Still she fought the urge to scoot away.

"This is better than sitting up," he said.

Maybe for him, but not for her. She wasn't used to sleeping with anyone not covered in fur.

"I'd hold you until you fell asleep, but that wouldn't be good for your head or your arm." Flynn rolled onto his side, facing her, and held her hand. "Whatever scared you was only a dream. You're not going to fall. You're safe."

She'd felt safe with Flynn earlier, but hearing him say the words sent a million thoughts about him running through her aching head. Not one of them made sense. The only logical thing for her to do was to sleep.

Or rather, try.

Anna closed her eyes and waited for sleep to come.

A cat jumped onto the bed. More followed until all five were on the bed with her and Flynn. He was on top of the covers. She was beneath them. But it was weird.

Milo took his spot between her feet.

Everyone was in bed. Her bed. The chills and goose bumps had disappeared. Flynn emanated heat better than the forced air through the floor registers.

Yet, she couldn't sleep. Tossing and turning might help, but moving hurt. She lay on her back with her eyes closed, trying not to think about anything, especially the hottie surgeon next to her, still holding her hand.

"Stop thinking and sleep," Flynn whispered.

"How did you know I was awake?"

"I can hear you thinking." His voice held no judgment. "And that's not good, concussion or not."

He rubbed her hand with his thumb.

"What are you doing?" she whispered, which was silly. They were alone except for her fur babies, who must be grateful for an extra warm body to sleep against.

"Trying to get you to stop thinking. Is it working?"

"I'm not sure."

"Does it feel good?"

Better than good. "Yes."

"Then I won't stop." He squeezed her hand before continuing to rub with his thumb. "Now sleep."

Easier said than done, but Anna would try. If not for her sake, then for his.

SUNLIGHT FILTERED THROUGH the blinds. Anna blinked open her eyes. The natural light wasn't bright enough to make her head hurt. Progress? She hoped so.

The warm temperature in the room felt more like a summer morning than a spring one. She'd kicked the covers off during the night. Someday, she would buy a portable air conditioner.

A cat purred. The feline motor engine sounded like Bristol.

Anna glanced toward the sound and saw…

Flynn.

A bare-chested Flynn.

A bare-chested Flynn, surrounded by her fur babies with his hand over her stomach and resting on her hip.

Her heart melted.

She'd appreciated him holding her hand while she fell asleep, but she never imagined waking up like this.

It didn't suck.

Cats surrounded his head and upper body. Anna never thought she'd be jealous of a cat, but she wouldn't mind being curled up next to Flynn, too. Though she couldn't complain.

Milo, the cutie, slept between her and Flynn, spread out on his back with his feet in the air as if he didn't have a care in the world.

Anna had no idea where her cell phone was. She hadn't seen it since the day of the shower, but she wasn't supposed to use any electronics. Still she would have loved to take a photo of Flynn.

Not for blackmail.

Though, she had a feeling his family would be surprised that he'd turned into Dr. Dolittle, albeit a sleeping one. But Anna wanted a photograph for her, to remember the moment and him.

She didn't want to blink in case she was dreaming again.

Milo's paws twitched. He must be the one who was dreaming.

Snowy meowed.

"Shhhh." Anna didn't want the cat to wake Flynn, even

though it had to be breakfast time.

Midge stretched, so did Inky.

Flynn opened his eyes. He did a double take and grinned. "Oh, good morning."

"Hey."

He lifted his hand off her. "Sleep well?"

She nodded. "You?"

"I did." He glanced at the cats staring at him. "Though based on the glares I'm getting it appears I slept in."

"You recognize the I'll-die-of-starvation-if-you-don't-feed-me-now vibe." Snowy flipped her tail as if she'd heard Anna. "Don't worry. They'll survive until you're ready to get up. Figured you didn't want me to do it."

"Too soon for that." He studied her. "Your eyes are brighter today. Your complexion isn't as pale."

She tilted her face to show him the left side. "Is the bruise better?"

"Getting there."

She knew what that meant. "You're being polite."

"Bruises look worse before they get better. That's how they heal." He counted the animals. "Five cats and one dog."

"Huh?"

"Need to make sure I don't startle anyone when I get up."

Okay, that was sweet. He was sweet. And yes, her crush was growing.

He sat and, despite her head hurting, Anna enjoyed the view. Flynn might work all the time, but he was fit.

He swung his feet off the bed. "I should grab a shower

before Taryn arrives with breakfast. Though I'll feed the cats first, so they don't bother you."

The doorbell rang.

Milo bolted upright. He barked, jumped off the bed, and ran out of the room.

"That must be her." He stood. "I'll answer it."

"Taryn's your sister-in-law, but you might want to put on a shirt. I doubt she'd mind, but the neighbors might...talk."

Who was Anna kidding? News of a shirtless man answering her door in the morning would spread through Silver Falls like wildfire. She didn't want Flynn to be the subject of gossip. Herself, either.

"I'll grab a shirt." He hesitated. "You're okay this morning?"

"My head and arm still hurt."

Flynn brushed his hand through his hair. "No, I mean..."

The doorbell rang again.

"I'm fine." Anna didn't know if he was worried about him sleeping with her, but she was fine. Confused about her feelings toward him, but he wasn't the first man she'd been attracted to who didn't feel the same way about her. He wouldn't be her last. "Taryn has a key she'll use if you don't answer."

That got him moving.

Less than a minute later, Milo stopped barking, which meant Taryn must be inside.

Anna reached for her water bottle and sipped.

Voices sounded, but they were muted. She didn't need to hear what they said. Not when her head still felt foggy, though more cotton balls instead of a damp rag inside her skull. And her arm…

She hoped it was only a sprain. A cast would be a literal pain. That reminded her. She needed to make a doctor's appointment.

Taryn, dressed in her bakery whites minus the hairnet and hat, entered the bedroom. "How are you feeling today?"

"Better."

"Is Doctor Flynn taking care of you?"

Anna's face felt warm. "Yes."

Taryn's gaze narrowed. "Are you blushing?"

Probably, but… "It's hot in here."

"Well, you know those Andrews brothers. All three are hot."

Heat pooled in Anna's cheeks. "Taryn."

"What?" Taryn held out her hands. "It's true. Keaton's geeky gorgeous. Flynn's got fashion model features. But I'm partial to my ruggedly handsome husband."

She wasn't wrong, but Anna found Flynn more attractive than his brothers.

Taryn came to the side of the bed. "Flynn mentioned you wanted a shower. He thought you'd be more comfortable with my help than his."

Relief flooded Anna. "I would be. Thanks."

Taryn pulled her cell phone from her pants pocket and glanced at the screen. "You're in luck. I don't have to be at the bakery for another thirty minutes. Plenty of time to help you. Your doctor's appointment is at ten."

"This morning?"

Taryn nodded. "Margot and my mother-in-law made some calls yesterday."

"So they called on a Sunday? And got me an appointment?"

"Those two women are unstoppable. Garrett's dad is great, but his mom is the one who keeps everything running from the hospital where she works to their family."

"You like your mother-in-law."

"I do. She's tough on her kids, but she's also a mama bear. I have nothing but respect for the woman, who gave birth to and raised my husband." Taryn glanced at the door. "I sent Flynn out to walk Milo. He looked like he could use some fresh air and sunshine."

Guilt coated Anna's mouth. "I had a nightmare last night and woke him up."

"He'll catch up on his rest soon enough. That's why he's in Silver Falls." Taryn motioned to the pillow next to Anna and grinned. "Though it looks like someone had a sleepover last night."

Anna's entire face burned. "I couldn't fall back asleep and…"

"You don't have to explain, but I'm glad Flynn's stepping up."

"He should be taking care of himself."

"Once Margot gets her hands on him again, she'll make sure he rests." Taryn came closer to the bed. "It's all good. And you'll feel better after a shower."

Anna would, except she wished she didn't miss Flynn so much. A crush was one thing, but it was more than that. She was falling for him. Normal under the circumstances, right? He was her caretaker. That must elicit certain…feelings. She only hoped she didn't fall too hard.

Healing a head and arm would be hard enough. She didn't want to add her heart into the mix. Though she got the sinking feeling it might be too late.

Chapter Fifteen

A S FLYNN DROVE Anna home after her doctor's appointment, he kept glancing at her in the passenger seat. She seemed fine after the visit, if not a little tired, but Flynn was worried. Doctor Rosen appeared competent, but he'd been so friendly with Anna. More like a pal than her physician.

Flynn hadn't liked that. "Have you been a patient of Dr. Rosen's for long?"

"No. My doctor retired, and she recommended him. I don't get sick that much. I see him more on First Avenue than at his office."

That could explain the friendliness. Emphasis on could. "You're lucky to be so healthy."

She nodded. "Doctor Rosen started a weekend urgent care clinic, which has been a blessing to Silver Falls. Not every injury or illness needs a hospital, so it's come in handy for locals wanting to avoid the ER and much cheaper, too."

Flynn forgot she had to consider the cost of medical care. Something he'd never had to do. "That's nice."

But Flynn still was iffy on the doctor's professionalism. Silver Falls might be a small town, but Dr. Rosen wasn't much older than Anna. Maybe he was interested in her or vice versa.

Flynn tightened his grip on his rental car's steering wheel.

"Thanks for driving me to my appointment. I'm relieved my arm is only sprained." Anna showed off her new brace that strapped on with Velcro. "I can move my fingers in this. I'll still need help washing dogs, but I should be able to groom them with no problem."

Flynn had asked to see the X-ray, much to the chagrin of Dr. Rosen's staff, but he was only being cautious. Anna needed both hands for grooming dogs. Thankfully, the diagnosis had been correct. With the decreased swelling in her forearm, the imaging showed no fractures.

"Yes, but you heard what Doctor Rosen said," Flynn reminded her. "Be careful, or you'll end up wearing the brace for a long time. He wants you to take this week off and not go in until Monday."

"I was hoping I'd heard that wrong, but I'll follow the rules. I also don't want to end up with that other thing he mentioned." She shuddered. "Post-concussion syndrome."

"You don't." Which was why Flynn hadn't appreciated Dr. Rosen telling Anna that she would be fine on her own after tomorrow. That seemed way too soon. "I can stay a few more days to make sure you're okay."

"Doctor Rosen said I would be fine. There's the meal train, so I won't have to cook all week."

Flynn didn't feel comfortable leaving her until he knew she was healed. "It's no trouble."

"You need to focus on your recovery. I don't want to be the reason you're stuck in Silver Falls longer than you have to be. I know how much your job means to you."

Flynn didn't mind, but she made a valid point. No matter how much he enjoyed spending time with Anna, he wasn't there to play doctor, rather caretaker, for anyone except himself. His goal was to return to L.A.

How had he lost sight of that?

The answer struck lightning-bolt fast.

Because Anna was special. He'd never met anyone like her. That gave him an idea. "We should make the most of tonight since it's my last one with you."

"You mentioned going out the day of the shower." She sounded pleased with herself for remembering. "We can do that tonight. Dinner is coming from the Falls Café."

"You like staying home."

"I do. Margot thinks you and Pippa are a perfect match, but this will keep any gossip from circulating."

He grimaced. "Margot thinks you and Dr. Idiot would be good together."

"Who?" Anna asked.

Flynn swallowed. "Sorry, Dr. Wingate."

"Oh."

Oh? What did that mean? Flynn glanced her way. "Would you go on a date with him?"

"We met under weird circumstances. I don't remember him all that well. So…maybe."

Grrr. Flynn wanted to hear *no*. N-O. But *maybe* was better than *yes*.

Anna yawned.

She must be tired. "Do you want dinner in bed, or do you feel up to eating at the table?"

"If I take a nap, I should be good to eat at the table."

"Then it's off to bed as soon as we get home." He realized what he'd said. "Get you home."

Once there, he helped Anna into the house with his arm around her in case she got dizzy, even though her balance appeared to have improved since yesterday.

The cats were nowhere in sight, but Milo greeted them with barks and a wagging tail. He darted for Anna's legs.

Flynn scooped up the dog with his free hand. "Let's make sure your mom gets to her bedroom safely. Then I'll let you down."

The dog panted happily.

"You spoil him." Anna sounded amused not angry. "Milo's a creature of habit. One time makes a habit for him. He'll expect you to carry him from now on."

Milo licked his hand. The dog was kind of cute. "Not a problem. He's light."

Flynn followed Anna into her bedroom. She sat on the bed and kicked off her slip-on shoes.

He placed Milo on the bed since the dog would want to be next to Anna. "Need help?"

"I'm getting better at doing things with only one hand."

She was, but Flynn fought the urge to help her with the comforter.

She grinned proudly. "See?"

"Great job." Flynn only wanted to make things easier on

her, but he also wanted to kiss her good night, even though she was only napping. He brushed his fingers through his hair. "Sleep well."

"Take a nap, too. You must be tired."

He was. "I will."

But first he wanted to make plans for dinner. Anna had been through so much, she deserved a nice date tonight, even if it was one at home.

A KNOCK SOUNDED. Flynn had been proactive and put Milo in the backyard to keep the dog's barks from waking Anna. Flynn had checked on her a few minutes ago, and she was sound asleep with a soft smile on her pretty face. He stepped around Inky, sprawled across the floor. None of the cats seemed to mind him being around. He hoped that made things easier for Anna.

Flynn opened the front door. Callie held a brightly colored flower arrangement.

He smiled. "You picked a pretty one."

"You asked for something pretty." She made her way inside. "What's going on with you and Anna?"

"Nothing."

Callie shot him an I-don't-believe-you look. "You asked me to pick up a flower arrangement Anna would like. That's not nothing."

"Tonight's dinner is being delivered from the Falls Café. After the shower I asked Anna if she wanted to go out, and so we're doing that tonight."

The word sounded strange coming off his lips. Strange, but right.

Callie's nose scrunched. "You and Anna are going on a date?"

"At home. Well, her home."

He didn't know why he kept making that mistake. His house was three times the size of hers. Though his was lots of glass and empty walls, not much personality. He hadn't unpacked all the boxes after living there for a few years. But he would do that when he got back to L.A. Creating a home like Anna had would be part of him finding balance.

Callie tilted her head. "You don't like Anna."

"I didn't know her."

"Pippa's your type, not Anna."

Callie's words shocked him. "Do you not want this dinner date to happen? If that's the case, you have to tell Anna. I won't hurt her that way."

Callie's jaw dropped. "You like her."

"You just said I didn't like her."

"No, I mean you like *like* her."

He loved Callie, but sometimes she made no sense. "I'm still tired, can you simplify whatever you're talking about and explain it as if I were a child?"

She tilted her head. "You know how some seven-year-old boys are mean to girls at school."

That was over thirty years ago. "Not really."

Callie straightened a yellow rose in the arrangement. "Well, sometimes a boy will pull a girl's ponytail or call her a mean name or blatantly ignore her."

"That's bullying."

"It's also how some boys deal with crushes—or they used to. I hope they've evolved from that."

"What does any of this have to do with me and Anna?"

"I think you've had a crush on Anna since you first came to Silver Falls the Christmas before last. That's why you haven't been nice to her."

Huh? Clearly Callie was confused. "First, I was never not nice. I might have been dismissive, but I was never mean or a bully."

Her lips pursed the same way they had when she was younger and trying to make a point. "You hired an investigator to do a background check on her and suggested she was out to scam me."

"A good thing I did," Flynn shot back. "Garrett needs to find a better person since the guy failed to discover Anna's old name."

Callie inhaled sharply. She bobbled the flowers, but he grabbed them so they didn't crash to the floor.

"What?" he asked.

"Anna told you about her past?" Callie whispered.

"Er, yes." He wasn't sure what she knew about Anna's past, so he didn't want to repeat any specifics.

"Anna must like you, too." Callie went into the living room and plopped onto the couch. "I don't know if this is the most wonderful thing in the world or the worst."

Her confused tone made no sense. He set the flowers on the table. "Why the worst? She's your best friend."

"Yes, but you're the godparents to our baby."

"Still not seeing the problem."

"What if you date, and it doesn't work out? We'll have to keep you and her apart at every family event. The tension will keep thickening until even the baby notices. At some point, it'll get so bad the two of you will have to alternate who attends what. It'll be a disaster. A total catastrophe."

Flynn held up his hands, palms facing Callie. "Slow down, baby sis. You're getting ahead of yourself. This is only one dinner."

"Between two people who've spent nearly seventy-two hours together if we count setting up the baby shower. Broken up into chunks of time, that would equal many dates. For some, it would add up to an entire relationship."

"We were asleep for some of that."

"Except you slept next to her in the hospital and shared a bed last night."

It wasn't a question. Frustration knotted his shoulder muscles.

Silver Falls had no secrets. Taryn must have figured where he slept last night. Given how worried Anna was about the neighbors seeing him shirtless and in his pajama bottoms, she wouldn't have mentioned sharing a bed to anyone.

"Anna had a nightmare," he explained calmly, not wanting to add fuel to a grill of glowing briquets. "Nothing happened."

"I hope not since Anna has a concussion and an injured arm." Callie didn't sound pleased. She crossed her arms over her chest.

Outside, Milo scratched at the back door. Flynn let him in.

The dog ran straight to Callie and jumped onto the couch. She uncrossed her right arm and rubbed him.

"I'm not against tonight's dinner," she said finally. "But please be careful. You know how Pippa didn't want to date casually. Anna's the same way. She'll want more or think this is more or—"

"We ate dinner together last night, and Anna didn't blow that up into something it wasn't."

Callie raised a brow. "Did you go to all this trouble?"

"Flowers aren't trouble, but no. We ate on her bed."

"A picnic in bed. That's so sweet. And romantic."

His sister had a strong case of happy couple syndrome. A chronic infliction they hoped to infect friends and family with. The disease was curable only with a breakup or divorce. "Are all newlyweds this sappy?"

"I have no idea what you're talking about." She motioned to the floral arrangement. "Back to Anna. I see a tablecloth on the table. That wasn't there yesterday. I doubt Anna put that out, given her injuries."

"I want the dinner to be nice. That's why I asked for flowers to go on the table." He didn't understand Callie's concern. "Would you rather I grab burgers and fries from that local fast-food place you like so much?"

A beat passed. "Anna deserves better."

"Exactly."

Callie bit her lip. "No, I mean, Anna deserves a man who plans to stick around Silver Falls, not bolt out of town as soon as he feels better and can return to work."

Her works sank in. She couldn't have been clearer. "You think a dinner date is a bad idea."

Callie took a deep breath and exhaled even longer. "I love you both, but yes, I do. It's like watching a trainwreck you know will happen. But for this one, I want to look away. I know your track record, and I know Anna's."

"That's not fair," he said for both his and Anna's sakes. "You make it sound as if we'll be engaged and in divorce court the week after next. All I want to do is treat Anna to a special evening. Is that so wrong?"

"You're serious about it being only a dinner?"

"What else would it be?"

"A turn-on-the-charm full-court press to win her heart and undying affection?"

He wouldn't mind winning either, but now wasn't the time.

"Even if I wanted to do that, which I don't, Anna isn't up for a whirlwind romance. I'm going back to Margot's tomorrow. I can spoil Anna for one night." Flynn didn't want this to upset Callie. He didn't need her permission, but he would ask for it. "Is that okay for me to do this?"

"My gut says no, but Anna deserves a special night. She hasn't had one since—"

"Davis," Flynn growled.

"Anna must have let her guard down if she mentioned him, too."

"We're friends." Except the word tasted gritty in his mouth. "We've spent time together."

More than he'd spent with anyone except staff members at the hospital.

Tonight was only a dinner, but what Flynn didn't tell Callie was he hoped to spend more time with Anna once she felt better. He had a feeling his baby sis wouldn't like that, which was why Callie would never have to know.

Chapter Sixteen

THE THREE-COURSE DINNER with tomato bisque soup, baby greens and pear with candied walnut salad, and phyllo-wrapped salmon with grilled asparagus was delicious. Anna enjoyed every bite. The best part, however, wasn't the food or the mouthwatering chocolate layer cake from Lawson's Bakery Garrett had dropped off earlier.

Hands down, Anna's favorite was Flynn.

He'd dimmed the lights and placed votive candles from her bookcase on either side of a gorgeous flower arrangement that must've come from Pippa's shop. Somehow, he'd found a tablecloth and matching napkins. Anna couldn't remember the last time she'd used those. Flynn's effort made tonight special, made her feel special, too.

She leaned forward, wanting to bridge the table separating them. "Thank you for tonight. Everything was perfect."

He raised his glass of sparkling water. "Especially the company."

Heat pooled in her cheeks. She hoped he couldn't tell she'd fallen for him big-time. When they'd met a year ago December and a few times since, she'd seen him as an arrogant surgeon and Callie's overprotective oldest brother.

Anna hadn't known the real Flynn. She wanted to get to know him better.

"Thanks." Smiling was hard not to do even when her head hurt. "I didn't expect any of this."

"You deserve it."

She wanted to believe that. "Well, you get an A-plus for everything you've done for me."

"Let's sit on the couch." He stood and helped her stand.

His dress shirt and gold-striped tie brought out the amber in his eyes. So handsome. She'd felt underdressed in her leggings and oversized nightshirt, but they were easy to get on and off with only one hand. She hadn't wanted to wear pajamas for their dinner, and this was what she'd worn to Dr. Rosen's office.

"So attentive," she teased.

"As I said before, you deserve it."

"Be careful or I might swoon."

"I've got fast reflexes and excellent hands."

Her heart went pitter-patter. She better get to the couch before her knees gave out, and he needed to catch her. Funny thing was, she had no doubt he would.

Flynn helped her sit and took the spot on her right. "Now I don't have to worry about bumping your brace."

"My arm's not broken," she reminded him.

"Just want to be careful."

As she should be. But a part of her wanted to toss reason into the wind where Flynn Andrews was concerned and go for it.

The only question was what *it* meant. "We've discussed

every topic under the sun. I'm not sure how much more my brain can take."

"We can be quiet." He laced his fingers with hers. "I like holding your hand."

"I like it, too." Even if holding hands should feel childish, with Flynn, it felt…important. As if they fit together, and she hadn't felt that way with anyone. Oh, Anna had thought she felt that with Davis, but she'd been wrong.

No paws sounded on the floor. No cats meowed for treats. No Milo acted out, trying to be the center of attention.

The silence was good for her head, but she enjoyed the man seated next to her more. He'd helped her to the bathroom. He'd been there when she got nauseated. Both situations had been awkward. Maybe that explained why the quiet wasn't uncomfortable.

"Can I kiss you?" Anna hadn't known where the question sprung from. Most likely her heart. Her head still hurt, but she wasn't foggy or fuzzy-brained. She wanted to kiss Flynn, more than she'd wanted anything in a long time.

His eyes darkened as if he wanted to kiss her too, but he drew back slightly. "Your head."

"My head can stand a short kiss."

"Short?"

"Brief, not one with your hands in my hair and mine in yours smashing our mouths together like in the movies. Gentler would be better. Preferred."

"I agree with your prescription."

Anna wiggled her toes, even if her concussed brain told

her this might not be her smartest idea. She wanted—no, needed—to do this, even if it was the only kiss she ever got from Flynn. She needed to experience one.

"Ready?" he asked.

"Shouldn't I be asking you since the kiss is my idea?"

She pressed her mouth against his. His lips moved gently against hers with such tenderness tears filled her eyes.

It was a soft kiss, one that made her feel as special as the dinner tonight. She tasted his warmth and chocolate from the cake and a tang of salt, which must be him.

The kiss was sweet, and Anna leaned into him, never wanting it to end.

His arms went around her for an instant and then he loosened them and pulled away. "Sorry. I forgot about your injuries."

Her lips tingled. Pleasurable sensations shot through her. "You have nothing to apologize for."

"Then thank you for coming up with the wonderful idea to kiss."

Her smile spread. "Thank you for kissing me back."

Except thanks seemed inadequate when her response to his kiss left her wanting more...wanting him in life. Anna had found two things she'd never expected to find with Dr. Flynn Andrews—a sense of belonging and home.

"I..." they said at the same time.

Snowy ran around the living room doing a feline version of parkour.

He laughed. "So much for a quiet night alone."

"Never alone. At least not for long. Fur babies trick you

into thinking they're asleep for the night and then…" Anna yawned.

Flynn stood. "You've had a busy day. You must be tired."

She glanced at where they'd eaten. "The table—"

"I'll blow out the candles and put things away while Milo goes outside for the last time tonight." Flynn helped her stand. "Let's get you ready for bed."

A few minutes later, Anna was tucked in with the cats beside her. Milo wasn't there, so he must still be outside. She closed her eyes. But she was too keyed up to sleep.

All Anna saw was Flynn, front and center in her mind. She hoped he played a starring role in her dreams.

Paws sounded against the floor.

Anna opened her eyes. Flynn stood next to the bed in his sleep pants and a T-shirt. "Do you think you'll have nightmares tonight?"

"I might."

"I don't mind sleeping on top of the covers again, if you think it'll help you."

"It would help." She didn't need time to think about it. "Would you hold my hand?"

"Of course."

He got into bed, careful not to disturb the cats, but Bristol and Pumpkin moved. Milo stood on the corner of the mattress as if waiting until everyone took their place so he could find his.

So unlike her "extra" dog, but Anna wouldn't complain.

Flynn lay on his side facing her, took hold of her hand

and kissed the top of it.

She had a feeling of déjà vu.

He lowered their linked hands to the mattress. "Sweet dreams."

"You, too, Flynn." Anna wanted to enjoy this for as long as she could. Which was only until tomorrow. But that was more than she'd had, so it would be enough.

It had to be.

ANNA WOKE ALONE. Her bed had never felt so empty. Her water bottle had been refilled, and something smelled good. She sat on the edge of the bed.

Pancakes? Maybe French toast?

Whatever was cooking made her mouth water.

Anna didn't feel as foggy this morning, but she also didn't want to do something stupid to set her recovery back. "Flynn?"

Footsteps sounded, but not his.

"Oh, you're awake." Margot sashayed into the room. "You look better than you did on Sunday morning."

"Thanks. Where's Flynn?"

"I sent him on a walk with Milo. Told him to stop by Raine's for coffee." Margot's blue eyes twinkled. "I might have also suggested Pippa go by the coffee shop with a flower to give you."

"I got flowers yesterday."

"Callie got them for you."

Callie, not Flynn? A funny feeling settled in the pit of

Anna's stomach. But something didn't make sense. "I have flowers. Why do I need another one?"

"Oh, dear." Margot patted her hand. "If I didn't know you had a concussion, I'd know now."

"You lost me."

"So sorry." Margot beamed as if her quilt had won the blue ribbon at the county fair. "Now that he's finished taking care of you, we can get him to see Pippa's perfect for him. Everyone, including his siblings, agree. He needs a reason to stick around Silver Falls and not go back to L.A. What better reason than love?"

"All his siblings agree?"

"Yes, especially Callie."

The room tilted. Anna clutched the comforter.

Lines deepened Margot's face. "The color drained from your face. Are you okay?"

"I'm sorry." Anna didn't know why she was apologizing. "I need to go back to bed for a little bit." That wasn't a lie, but her bedroom was the only place she could be alone.

Margot helped her get under the covers. "Should I call Flynn?"

"No." Anna wouldn't know what to say to him. "I just need some rest."

"I'm cooking breakfast. You have plenty of time for a nap. I'll text Flynn and tell him not to rush back. That'll give him more time to visit with Pippa."

Anna's stomach churned. "You're living up to being Silver Falls's Cupid."

"That I am." Pride dripped from each word. "And I'm

never wrong. I can't wait to prove to everyone Pippa will be a perfect doctor's wife. And for you to go out with Doctor Wingate. You'd be a perfect doctor's wife, too."

Except the only doctor Anna wanted was Flynn.

She fought the urge to throw the covers over her head. Instead, she squeezed her eyes shut so she wouldn't cry and pretended to fall asleep.

THE DOOR OPENED and closed. The scent of whatever had been cooking disappeared, but Anna's bladder wouldn't let her stay in bed any longer.

Dr. Rosen had said she would be fine on her own, so she would take him at his word. Slowly, she walked to the bathroom. She had no trouble going through her morning routine.

After brushing her teeth and hair, Anna glanced at herself in the mirror. The reflection that greeted her was one hundred percent dog groomer, a woman who'd escaped a horrific childhood. She might have overcome her upbringing and she took pride in healing the scars of her past, but no one, not even her best friend, would ever see someone different. Or picture Anna with a man like Flynn.

You knew this.

Anna did. But something had changed once she got to know Flynn and let him get to know her.

She straightened.

No biggie.

All she had to do was survive this morning. He was leaving today. If his coffee with Pippa went well, he might not pick up his stuff until later.

On that pleasant thought, Anna opened the door.

Flynn stood in the hallway with Milo at his feet. "Margot said you needed to go back to bed. Is it your head?"

My heart. "I wanted to rest some more."

"Did you sleep okay last night?"

"I slept fine."

"So did I."

"You were gone when I woke up."

"Margot." Flynn shook his head. "She's playing match-maker again."

Anna shouldn't ask, but when had that stopped her? "How'd it go?"

He eyed her warily. "Let's get you some breakfast. You must be hungry."

Not really. Still Anna followed him to the table and sat. The flowers were the ones from last night. The ones Callie had picked out.

Anna sighed.

Flynn went into the kitchen. A minute later, he set a plate in front of her. "French toast and bacon. You should avoid caffeine until your head feels better. Will a cup of herbal tea do?"

She nodded. "Or water."

He brought her tea along with a plate for himself.

Anna took a few bites to avoid any questions.

"This tastes so good." Flynn wiped his mouth. "Want more?"

"I'm done, thanks."

"Do you want to go back to bed or are you up for sitting on the couch? I want to talk to you about something."

Oh, boy. She hoped this wasn't about Pippa, but what else could it be?

Anna swallowed around the lump in her throat. "The couch is fine."

He helped her over and sat next to her, the same as last night. She doubted there would be another kiss.

Had he kissed Pippa this morning after their coffee date?

Ugh. Anna felt as if she were on one of those reality TV dating shows. She didn't like the jealousy welling inside her. She should be happy for Pippa and Flynn.

"I'm packed, but before I leave, I want you to know how much I enjoy spending time with you." Flynn held her hand.

Wait. Anna stared at their linked fingers. Why was he holding her hand when he was with Pippa?

"I don't know how long I'll be in Silver Falls, but I want to keep seeing you," he continued. "This might be a little soon, but I'm going to say it anyway. I want to keep seeing you when I go back to L.A."

Anna did a double take.

"What?" he asked.

"You're not dating Pippa now?"

"No." Realization seemed to dawn. He blew out a breath. "Margot mentioned her matchmaking plan."

"She did."

"I had coffee with Pippa and didn't accept the flower she'd brought me. You have the ones I asked Callie to get for last night. That was it." He smiled at Anna. "If I haven't made myself clear, I want to date you."

Joy overflowed from Anna's heart. She wanted that, too. Except...

Pippa's perfect for Flynn. Everyone, including his siblings, agree.

All his siblings agree?

Yes, especially Callie.

The words looped in Anna's head, but it wasn't only that. "I don't want a long-distance relationship."

"Long distance is hard. I get it. Come to L.A."

Wait. He couldn't mean... "To visit?"

"To live."

She stiffened. Every nerve ending went on alert.

"Move to L.A.," he continued. "We can form a partnership and set you up with your own grooming business."

"A...partnership?"

Flynn grinned. "You'd be a great business investment."

He wasn't looking for a wife, let alone a girlfriend. He wanted someone to hang out with and keep him company when he wasn't working at the hospital. Someone who could also be a business partner.

His family thought Pippa was perfect for him. Flynn didn't, but he didn't see Anna as perfect for him either. Okay, he wanted to date her, but there'd been no declaration of feelings other than she'd make a great business investment.

She shivered.

This wasn't how she wanted things to be with him. The truth smacked into her the way her head must have hit the floor when she fell. Even if he'd said the three words she longed to hear, the three words she'd been dreaming about hearing since she was old enough to know what they meant, she wasn't returning to California.

Not to date.

Not for a business opportunity.

Not even for what she wanted most in this world—love.

Flynn leaned toward her. His smile was eager, like a puppy. "What do you say?"

"Thank you, but no."

He drew back as if stunned. "Why not?"

"I told you about my past. I don't want to go back to California."

"I have money. I can protect you if your father—"

"I want to stay in Silver Falls."

Hurt showed on his expression. "My life is in L.A."

"Mine is here." She wasn't sorry for saying that.

This was for the best. For him and his family and for her. Anna only wished it didn't hurt so bad. Because it did.

His eyes implored her. "There has to be a way for us to work out."

"How?" It was an honest question. "Our lives are in different cities, different states."

"I want to see if what we have could turn into more."

"And then what?"

He stared at her as if she'd lost her mind. Maybe she had to be turning him down, but…

"We'd just end up having this same conversation about you wanting me to move."

"California isn't a bad place."

"I'm sorry, but my memories from there are living nightmares."

Flynn started to speak then stopped himself. He stood. "I'll get my suitcase."

Anna went to the front door and waited for him.

Flynn rolled the suitcase behind him.

A lump the size of one of Milo's tennis balls burned in her throat. She hated to see Flynn go. She swallowed. "Thank you. I needed your help more than I realized."

Something flashed in his eyes, but it disappeared before she could figure out what it was.

"You're welcome." His jaw jutted forward. "If you change your mind about dating…"

"I like you, Flynn, but my life is here." Her voice cracked. "When I left Southern California, I promised myself I wouldn't return."

"Promises can be broken."

The hope in his voice tore at her heart. She was tempted. But for what?

A few dates and a chance to own a grooming shop with someone who'd said they didn't have time for a relationship. L.A. might be one of the biggest cities in the country, but that didn't mean she would remain anonymous there. She wouldn't risk the life she'd built in Silver Falls. She couldn't, even if being with him felt right. Right except for the fact his family pictured him with someone else and he would be walking out her door in the next five minutes.

Out her door but not out of her life.

That was the kicker.

She would see Flynn whenever he returned to Silver Falls for visits or to spend a holiday with his family, at the baby's birthdays and milestone events, and one day he would return with a woman, maybe even a wife.

Pippa?

That would make his family happy.

As for Anna… Someday she hoped to have a person with her at those same events.

And face it. She'd been here before.

Flynn was no different from Davis, who'd wanted Anna on his terms—to date him nonexclusively. Flynn wanted her on his terms—in Los Angeles.

She was making the right decision for herself.

Anna Kent wasn't running from her past. Evie Mallory, the girl she'd once been, had been destroyed by the same drugs that ruined her parents' lives. May little Evie rest in peace with the woman who'd given birth to her. Anna needed to keep herself safe in the present so she could have the future she dreamed about. A future she deserved, no matter what anyone else thought.

If someone didn't understand that, they didn't get her.

Didn't love her.

Anna would keep the memory of Dr. Flynn Andrews tucked safely away in a portion of her heart. Their brief time together had set the bar for what she wanted. She wouldn't find another man exactly like him. But someone…close.

And Anna knew in her heart of hearts, all she had to do was continue to be patient.

Because he was out there.

Somewhere.

And they would be together. No matter how long she had to wait.

Chapter Seventeen

TWO WEEKS HAD passed since Flynn had left Anna's house. Two weeks of healing. Two weeks of missing him. But she was better and working, albeit with a helper for shampooing the dogs. But she was getting faster. Soon she would be back to full speed.

Anna parked in front of Taryn's house for a girls' night. That meant takeout and a rom-com film, though three of the four of them were living their own happily ever, but seeing her friends all together would be nice. They hadn't been in one place since the baby shower. Strike that, the hospital to see her. Everyone had been busy. Well, not Anna.

She carried two bottles of sparkling cider she'd purchased for the night.

Anna hadn't been a complete hermit. She'd taken Midge and Inky to an adoption event yesterday, but no one had wanted the bonded pair, so they'd come home with her. She still had some headaches and the stupid brace on her left arm, but she was improving every day.

Anna rang the doorbell.

Taryn answered. "I figured it was you or the pizza."

"No Chinese food tonight?"

"Certain smells bother Callie still, so I figured pizza was a safer choice."

Inside, her friends sat on the couch and in the chairs. She noticed two empty spots. One must be for her and the other for Taryn. Pippa sat next to Callie.

No big deal.

Anna didn't need to show her claws or teeth. She'd told Flynn no. He should find someone else who could make him happy. "I brought some bubbly our future baby mama can drink."

"Thanks." Callie motioned to the empty seat closest to her. "It's good to see you outside of Wags and Tails. You must be feeling better."

Taryn took the bottles into the kitchen.

"I am." Anna sat and studied her best friend. "Each day you look more radiant."

"One of the perks about pregnancy—to make up for the other things like having to go to the bathroom every seven minutes," Callie joked.

Everyone laughed.

"We're glad you're feeling better," Raine said. "I miss seeing you in the coffee shop."

"Not quite ready for caffeine." Anna missed her favorite drinks. "But soon. I go back to the doctor's next week, so I'll see what Dr. Rosen says."

"He's so cute." Pippa sipped an iced tea. "Which is why I go to a doctor in Summit Ridge. I can't imagine crushing on my doctor."

Oh, boy. Anna didn't know how to respond. "Dr. Rosen

is a nice guy."

"He stops by the shop every morning between eight and eight thirty," Raine said. "Not trying to usurp Margot's role as town matchmaker, but just thought you should know."

Pippa sighed. "I wish Margot would stop trying to force me and Flynn together."

Anna straightened.

"Just tell her no more matchmaking, if you're not interested," Callie suggested.

Pippa stared into her iced tea. "I'm not sure what I am."

Anna wanted to leave. As she prepared to stand and make an excuse, Taryn came out of the kitchen with two flutes of apple cider.

The baker handed one to Anna and the other to Callie.

"My favorite." Callie grinned and raised her glass. "To my Silver Falls family, especially Anna, my sister from another mother, who knows what I love and is the backbone of Wags and Tails. I couldn't keep the place running without you."

"To our Silver Falls family," the others replied.

Anna's breath hitched. For so long, she'd wanted to find family. But these women were her family. So were the people she worked with at the doggy daycare. Not family by blood, but family of the heart. They'd stepped up when she'd been hurt, brought her food, did whatever she needed to be done. That was what family did.

"Hey." Callie leaned closer to Anna and spoke softly. "You okay?"

She took a quick sip. "Actually, I am."

"Have you talked to Flynn?"

"No."

"You liked him."

"He's better off with someone like Pippa." Anna kept her voice low.

"That's not going to happen. He can't wait to get back to L.A."

"It's his home."

"No, it's where he lives. Home is where his heart is, but he hasn't figured out where that is yet."

Anna took another sip. "I hope he does. Flynn's a good man. He deserves to be happy."

Callie lowered her glass. "So do you."

"I will be." One of these days. "So did you finish the nursery?"

AS ONE MISERABLE day led to another, Flynn didn't do much except sleep. Margot's blatant matchmaking of him and Pippa had forced him to move into Callie and Brandt's house. Dr. Rosen, who wasn't such a bad guy after all, had given Flynn a physical and the authorization Mom required for him to return to work.

Flynn loaded his suitcase into the rental car's trunk. He'd said his goodbyes to Garrett, Taryn, Keaton, Raine, Margot, Brandt, and Callie last night. Yet Flynn hadn't been able to get in the car and drive to the airport the way he'd planned. He went back into the house.

Callie sat at her desk with Rex nearby on the floor. Her

due date was a month away, and she worked more from home these days. She wore a large T-shirt, leggings, and striped fuzzy socks with grippers on the bottom. Her hair was piled on top of her head in a messy bun. Her face was bare of makeup, and her tongue stuck out the way it had when she was a little girl. She was radiant. Beautiful.

More than a year ago when he came to Silver Falls to celebrate Christmas, Callie had shown her family she was a successful small-business owner, forging a place for herself in a new community two states away. He'd been proud of her. Now...

His baby sister was all grown up.

Logically, he'd known that she was getting older with every passing birthday, but he finally felt it in his heart. Flynn and the others might want to protect Callie the way they had since she was born, but she could take care of herself. She needed their love and support more than she needed them telling her what to do all the time.

Callie had created a professional and a personal life in Silver Falls, not letting anyone—including her family—get in the way of what *she* wanted. Flynn was happy for her but envious, a way he'd never expected to feel.

She closed the laptop and picked up a book.

Flynn squinted to read the title. Something about raising kind kids. He had to smile. The baby inside her ever-expanding stomach had won the parent lottery.

"You don't need that parenting book." Flynn approached her. "You and Brandt are two of the kindest people I know. Your kid, and future ones, will learn by the example you set."

Callie rested a hand on her stomach. "I want to be the best mom I can be."

Flynn motioned to the dog. "You already are. Look how happy and content Rex is. You'll do as well with a two-legged kiddo as a four-legged one."

"Thanks." She lowered the book. "I thought you'd be on your way to the airport by now."

"Packing took longer than I expected."

She glanced at her phone. Her forehead creased. "You're never going to make your flight."

"There are other planes."

Her gaze locked on his. "I don't think you want to leave."

I don't. The thought came so hard and fast, his breath stilled. What choice did he have? His job—his life—was in L.A. "I have to go home."

"Do you?"

Flynn shrugged. *Wrong answer.* But Callie made it sound as if he had a choice. He didn't. Not really.

"Yes, I do." His words carried no conviction. Not the way they should, given what he'd left behind—his job and his house and an entire life, everything he'd always wanted.

Except it's killing you.

Not any longer.

He'd rest so he was no longer tired. He'd learned his lesson. He would make some changes. His tendency was to go all-in, so balance wasn't a natural state for him, but he could find a way not to be so lopsided in his work versus personal life.

That worked well the last time, a voice mocked.

"I do," he repeated.

Callie tilted her head. "If that's the case, you'd be on your way to the airport."

He shifted positions, feeling more like a nervous school-boy than a highly respected surgeon.

"Why are you here with me when you want to be with Anna?" Callie asked.

Flynn flinched. He hadn't expected her to say that. He scratched his chin, not wanting to admit the truth, even to himself. But ignoring what had happened with Anna wouldn't change anything. Saying the words aloud might help him move on or at least get him into his car and to the airport, which was what he needed to do. He needed to do that.

He took a breath and then another. "Margot said you and everyone thought Pippa was the one for me."

"Margot sees what she wants to see. She's wrong in your case."

"It doesn't matter because Anna doesn't want me."

There. He'd said the words. The world hadn't stopped. But his chest hurt more. A lot more. He rubbed the left side of his chest.

Callie rolled her eyes. "Anna wants you, but she doesn't want to live in California."

"That's where I live and work."

Callie shook her head. "You're just like Davis."

"No, I'm not."

"Anna's always dated guys who only want to go out with

her on their terms."

"I never—"

"You asked her to move to L.A.," Callie interrupted. "I'm surprised you did, since you've never been that serious with anyone."

"Little good it did me."

"Some women would jump all over the chance, but not Anna. She wants—needs—someone who will love her unconditionally. Something she's never had in her life from a man. Not even from her parents. That means accepting her wanting to be a small-town dog groomer."

His jaw tensed. "I'm not trying to mold Anna. I asked her to move because L.A. is where I live and work. I offered to go into business with her. Set her up in her own dog grooming salon. I support what she does."

"Very generous of you. Did you tell her you love her?"

"No, it seemed too soon."

"Did you at least tell her you liked her?"

"I said I wanted to date her, so it was implied. I also mentioned she'd be a great business partner."

Callie rolled her eyes. "Except Silver Falls is where Anna lives and works."

"I'm established at the hospital. I own a house."

"Anna has clients and loves her duplex," Callie countered. "She might not own it, but the place is her home. You imagined the perfect way to have Anna with you. But try to see things from Anna's perspective."

He thought back. What Anna had told him about her past wove together in a tapestry, a clear visual of why she'd chosen the life she had. He'd wanted her with him, and like the other men in her life, it had been on his terms. He hadn't even considered hers.

Flynn's stomach sank. "You're right. I only thought about myself. Everything I offered was on my terms."

Callie lifted her chin. "What are you going to do about it?"

"I-I don't know." Other than begging for Anna to give him another chance. He scrubbed his face with his hand. "Have any ideas?"

"Figure out what matters most to you," Callie said. "Your job and living in L.A. or Anna?"

"Both are important."

"Sometimes you have to choose. Make one thing a priority in your life over everything else. Love has a way of helping you decide what's most important."

"Love?" The word rushed out. "Anna's priorities seem clear to me. I'm not one of them."

"She didn't want to give you an ultimatum."

"If Anna loved me…" Flynn couldn't believe he'd said the L-word. He took a breath. "If she did, it shouldn't matter where she lives or works."

Callie's gaze narrowed. "You believe that?"

"Yes." He didn't hesitate to answer.

"Then, wouldn't the reverse be true, too?"

Flynn stiffened. "What do you mean?"

"If you love Anna, does it matter where you live or work?"

As Callie's words sank in, his heart dropped lower and

lower. He was still putting everything on Anna. "I've been an arrogant surgeon."

It wasn't a question because he knew the answer.

"Yes, but you've always been one. And I say this with love, I'm not sure you can be any less arrogant than you are."

That made him laugh. "Point taken."

"But maybe it's time to be a smarter arrogant surgeon."

"You've been acting more like a big sister than my little one lately."

Callie's smile brightened her whole face. "I'm just your sister. No adjective required."

Flynn nodded. "Thanks for being my sis."

"I love you, Flynn. I only want what's best for you. The same as you want for me."

"You think you know what the best is."

Callie nodded. "If you follow your heart, which is what I hope you're ready to do, you'll know without a doubt."

As he left Callie and Brandt's house, Flynn used the airline's app on his phone to cancel his flight.

Flynn was a surgeon. He repaired or removed parts from people. He followed logic and science. He wasn't a cardiologist, but he knew how a heart functioned. Not, however, in the way Callie meant.

All the signs pointed to Anna. Somehow, he needed to show her that he wasn't like the other guys who'd come before him. He wanted to be better than them, be better than the man he'd been until meeting her.

He needed more than words to convince Anna. The question was what should he do?

Follow his heart.

Flynn only hoped his heart didn't mess this up more than he already had.

At Wags and Tails, Anna cleaned the grooming area after her final client. Her headaches had lessened significantly over the past weeks. Light no longer bothered her. She'd gotten used to the brace and could use her hand more. All was well, except…

Don't think about Flynn.

She was done with her appointments, but she couldn't leave until Becca got off school and arrived. Then, Anna planned to head home. She needed some time alone. The ache in her heart was still raw and hadn't healed the way her head and arm were healing. A pint of ice cream straight from the container might be the only thing to soothe the pain.

You made the right choice.

She had, but the words didn't help when happy couples were all she saw. To be honest, Anna was no longer sure she needed to be patient. She might not be meant to find love.

Squeak.

Anna turned. Milo trotted toward her with something red in his mouth.

"Where did you find that?" She dried her hands and took a closer look at the squeaky toy he carried. "Did someone give you a heart?"

"It only seemed right I give Milo a heart because you have mine."

Flynn.

Air rushed from her lungs. She glanced toward the doorway.

He stood in a pair of jeans and a button-down shirt. His hair was messy as if he'd been rushing. His face was flushed.

Her heart stuttered. "I thought you left."

"I'm supposed to be on a flight, but I couldn't leave."

Every muscle tensed. "Is Callie okay?"

"She's fine." He walked toward her, though strut was a better description.

Anna released the breath she'd been holding. "Then what are you doing here?"

"I couldn't leave Silver Falls. Something would be missing."

She bit her lip. "Your family."

"You."

Anna gasped. She hadn't expected him to say that.

He came closer, his eyes intent. "I'd miss you. I know how much Silver Falls means to you. And I'd rather stay here and be with you than anywhere else."

He looked like the same Flynn Andrews, but... "Who are you?"

The corners of his mouth lifted. "Arrogant surgeon, re member?"

She opened her mouth to speak, but no words came out.

"I was wrong, Anna," Flynn admitted. "I've spent so many years trying to save lives, but I haven't been living one myself. You showed me that, made me see so much about myself and what I need...want. And I want to spend what's left of my life with you."

Her pulse shot into the stratosphere. "Say what?"

He laughed. "I want to be the one kissing you under the mistletoe every December. Kissing you when the clock strikes midnight on New Year's Eve. And kissing you before we go to sleep every night."

"I'm speechless."

He came closer. "I want to be your person. And I want you to be mine."

Her vision blurred. "You're serious?"

He nodded. "Life hasn't always treated you kindly. I haven't either. I'm so sorry about that, but I'll do better."

Anna's heart pounded in her chest.

Flynn cupped her face with his hand. "I love you. And I love Milo, Bristol, Snowy, and Pumpkin. Inky and Midge, too."

Her heart soared. She never thought she'd hear someone say those words to her. Yes, they were just words, but the affection in Flynn's eyes and the tone of his voice told her they were true.

Emotion clogged the throat. Her eyes burned. At any moment, she might ugly cry, but she swallowed. "I love you."

His features relaxed slightly.

"Milo got a squeaky toy. I have toys for the cats in the car. This is for you." Flynn dropped onto one knee and pulled a ring box from his pocket. He opened it to show a sparkling diamond. "We can have a long engagement or a short one. Doesn't matter to me. Whatever you want. All I know is I want to spend the rest of my life with you. Marry me, Anna, please."

She covered her mouth with her hands.

Milo barked. He must have dropped the heart. She glanced at the dog, who picked up his new toy. It squeaked again.

Was Milo giving his approval? Not that she needed it because she knew.

Her patience had paid off.

"Yes." Anna sounded breathless, the way she felt. "I'll marry you."

Flynn slid the ring onto her finger, stood, and kissed her—a kiss full of hope, promise, and joy with a sprinkle of spring to give her a glimpse of the seasons they would spend together in the future.

Epilogue

December 31st...

THE ANNUAL NEW Year's Eve party at Margot's house was a roaring success. People filled the house, and a few hardy souls stood on the front porch watching the snow come down in blankets of white.

Anna stood at the buffet table eyeing the desserts. She couldn't decide which to try next, but the miniature éclairs looked good.

"You should have one of each." Callie came up with Brandt. The two held hands. "Don't you know there are no calories on national holidays?"

Brandt shook his head.

That was good enough for Anna. She grabbed an éclair. "How's Delaney?"

"She's sound asleep in the nursery with the dogs sleeping on the floor by the crib. She's part of their pack." Motherhood fit Callie, who smiled, no doubt thinking of her and Brandt's adorable daughter. "I still can't believe Margot set aside an entire room for her."

"She's already working on her wedding quilt," Anna teased.

"Stop," both parents said in unison. "We made Margot promise not to play matchmaker after she got Flynn's so-called perfect match wrong."

Anna smiled. "It worked out in the end, and Margot wasn't wrong about Pippa being a perfect doctor's wife."

Dr. Rosen had proposed to the florist on Christmas Day.

"But don't worry. Margot told me after Flynn and I got married, she was hanging up her matchmaking wand," Anna added.

Callie laughed. "I hope so but I'm not sure I believe her."

"Believe what?" Flynn came up to Anna and hugged her.

She shivered. "You're freezing. I thought you'd be at the hospital all night."

"And miss getting a kiss from my wife at midnight? No way."

Anna wiggled her toes. "Thank you."

In June, Flynn had sold his house in L.A. and moved to Silver Falls. He worked at Summit Ridge Hospital. His position allowed him to find the balance he needed and deserved. After getting married in a quaint but perfect in every way wedding in August, he'd moved into her duplex. They'd been so busy with wedding plans they hadn't figured out where to live yet.

Anna had no complaints. Her house truly was a home now.

And this Christmas, she'd gotten more kisses under the mistletoe than she could count, but she'd been willing to wait until next year for a New Year's Eve kiss. She was thrilled she wouldn't have to be patient. "What happened?"

Flynn winked. "I came up with a plan."

"Did it involve breath mints?" she teased, remembering last year.

"No, but we may be celebrating Valentine's Day with a special lunch instead of a dinner." Flynn caressed Anna's face. "I switched shifts with another doctor. Thought I might miss midnight with all the snow, but I followed a plow most of the way and made it in time."

He kissed her.

"Hey," Garrett shouted. "It's not midnight yet."

Taryn shook her head. "You know how newlyweds are."

"I sure do." Garrett kissed her.

"We can't take him anywhere." Keaton had his arm around Raine. "But that's a lawyer for you."

"I wouldn't mind a kiss." Raine grinned.

"You don't have to ask twice." Keaton kissed her.

Brandt kissed Callie.

Anna laughed. "Look what you started."

"I don't hear any complaints." Flynn held her hand.

Margot blew a noisemaker. "Let the countdown begin…"

"Five… Four… Three… Two… One…" the guests shouted.

Flynn kissed her hard on the lips. Anna relished the taste of him, even if he still was a little cold.

He rested his forehead against her. "Happy New Year, Mrs. Andrews."

A year ago, Anna had been alone when the clock struck midnight. She hadn't kissed Milo, though she'd given each dog in the puppy pile a scratch behind the ears.

Now, Anna not only had a husband, but also a dog and five cats. Flynn hadn't wanted Midge and Inky to leave, so they'd become foster failures. That was most likely the only time Flynn had taken pride in failing. And next year, her in-laws planned to retire and move to Silver Falls. The entire Andrews family would be in the same town.

No new pregnancies had been announced, but Keaton and Raine weren't reaching for flutes filled with champagne so maybe another Andrews was on the horizon.

Flynn handed her a glass of bubbly. "To at least sixty more New Year's Eves together."

"I like the sound of that." Anna tapped her glass against his and sipped.

One year had made all the difference. Her patience had paid off. She finally had the unconditional love she'd been wanting and waiting for. She'd already found the family she'd longed for thanks to Callie, Taryn, Raine, and Pippa.

Each had found their happily ever after in Silver Falls. And Anna couldn't wait to see what came next for all of them.

The End

Want more? Check out Keaton and Raine's story in
A Cup of Autumn!

Join Tule Publishing's newsletter for more great reads and weekly deals!

If you enjoyed *A Sprinkle of Spring*,
you'll love the other books in the...

Silver Falls series

Book 1: *The Christmas Window*

Book 2: *A Slice of Summer*

Book 3: *A Cup of Autumn*

Book 4: *A Sprinkle of Spring*

Available now at your favorite online retailer!

More Books by Melissa McClone

Ever After series

A pair of best friends, a prince looking for a bride, and an unexpected royal match… Could they all possibly live happily ever after?

Book 1: *The Honeymoon Prize*

Book 2: *The Cinderella Princess*

Book 3: *Christmas at the Castle*

Bar V5 Ranch series

The Bar V5 Ranch of Marietta, Montana: where love is found in the most unexpected places.

Book 1: *Home for Christmas*

Book 2: *Mistletoe Magic*

Book 3: *Kiss Me, Cowboy*

Book 4: *Mistletoe Wedding*

Book 5: *A Christmas Homecoming*

Available now at your favorite online retailer!

About the Author

With a degree in mechanical engineering from Stanford University, Melissa McClone worked for a major airline where she traveled the globe and met her husband. But analyzing jet engine performance couldn't compete with her love of writing happily ever afters. She's now a USA Today Bestselling author and has also been nominated for Romance Writers of America's RITA® award. Melissa lives in the Pacific Northwest with her husband, three children, a spoiled Norwegian Elkhound, and cats who think they rule the house. They do!

Thank you for reading

A Sprinkle of Spring

If you enjoyed this book, you can find more from all our great authors at TulePublishing.com, or from your favorite online retailer.

Made in the USA
Middletown, DE
14 May 2023

30567496R00146